Their Eyes Met...And Something Electrical Passed Between Them.

Something charged with so much force that it shocked every nerve in Harley's body to life. Mary Claire's nervous movements were as fleeting as those of a moth at a flame.

The brush of her fingers across his lips made Harley's heart do a slow somersault while his blood warmed in his veins. It had been a long time since a woman had touched him in such a way. He'd forgotten the tenderness, the comfort rendered in so simple a gesture. On a sigh, he caught her wrist in his hand then held her palm against his cheek, absorbing the softness of her skin.

Slowly the thundering of her pulse trapped beneath his fingers registered in his muddled mind, and Harley's gaze settled on lips slightly parted and eyes filled with... Was it longing?

D1007407

Dear Reader,

THE BLACK WATCH returns! The men you found so intriguing are now joined by women who are also part of this secret organization created by BJ James. Look for them in *Whispers in the Dark*, this month's MAN OF THE MONTH.

Leanne Banks's delightful miniseries HOW TO CATCH A PRINCESS—all about three childhood friends who kiss a lot of frogs before they each meet their handsome prince—continues with *The You-Can't-Make-Me Bride*. And Elizabeth Bevarly's series THE FAMILY McCORMICK concludes with *Georgia Meets Her Groom*. Romance blooms as the McCormick family is finally reunited.

Peggy Moreland's tantalizing miniseries TROUBLE IN TEXAS begins this month with *Marry Me, Cowboy*. When the men of Temptation, Texas, decide they want wives, they find them the newfangled way—they *advertise!*

A Western from Jackie Merritt is always a treat, so I'm excited about this month's *Wind River Ranch*—it's ultrasensuous and totally compelling. And the month is completed with *Wedding Planner Tames Rancher!*, an engaging romp by Pamela Ingrahm. There's nothing better than curling up with a Silhouette Desire book, so enjoy!

Regards,

Lucia Macro

Senior Editor

Please address questions and book requests to:
Silhouette Reader Service
U.S.: 3010 Walden Ave., P.O. Box 1325, Buffalo, NY 14269
Canadian: P.O. Box 609, Fort Erie, Ont. L2A 5X3

PEGGY MORELAND
MARRY ME, COWBOY

SILHOUETTE *Desire*
Published by Silhouette Books
America's Publisher of Contemporary Romance

To Jim Bob and Kelly Clayman of Windsong Farm in
Georgetown, Texas, who helped make this author's
childhood dream come true! Thanks for hours of riding
pleasure and for instilling in me the competitive edge
needed to race barrels and bend poles!

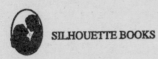 SILHOUETTE BOOKS

ISBN 0-373-76084-1

MARRY ME, COWBOY

Printed in U.S.A.

Books by Peggy Moreland

Silhouette Desire

A Little Bit Country #515
Run for the Roses #598
Miss Prim #682
The Rescuer #765
Seven Year Itch #837
The Baby Doctor #867
Miss Lizzy's Legacy #921
A Willful Marriage #1024
*Marry Me, Cowboy #1084

Silhouette Special Edition

Rugrats and Rawhide #1084

*Trouble in Texas

PEGGY MORELAND

published her first romance with Silhouette in 1989. She's a natural storyteller with a sense of humor that will tickle your fancy, and Peggy's goal is to write a story that readers will remember long after the last page is turned. Winner of the 1992 National Readers' Choice Award and a 1994 RITA finalist, Peggy frequently appears on bestseller lists around the country. A native Texan, she and her family live in Round Rock, Texas.

HARLEY KERR'S
THOUGHTS ON TEMPTATION, TEXAS!

I've lived my whole life in Temptation, a small town with an unlikely name in central Texas. Though there were those who considered living in Temptation a hardship and couldn't wait to escape, I've always loved it here and never gave a thought to leaving.

Since I was old enough to walk, I followed my father around the ranch, learning from his experience. I gleaned a ton of it on my own when I took over the place at the age of seventeen after his death. I fell in love when I was sixteen, married my high school sweetheart three years later and brought her home to my ranch.

Though I never gave it much consideration the first time around, I thought my expectations for a wife were simple enough. I wanted a woman I could love and care for, and one who was willing to love and care for me in return. She'd have to be a strong woman, someone who could stand the isolation of the land and still thrive, one who was both independent and dependent at the same time. I wanted a woman—a partner, if you will—who'd stand by me through thick and thin. I wanted, simply put, a home and a family and a woman to share it all with.

But my first wife didn't share those expectations. When we married, she was looking for a way out of Temptation, Texas. So when she left, taking my two kids with her, I sealed off my heart and swore never to love again.

When my old buddy, Cody Fipes, started this fool plan to advertise for women to move to Temptation to save our dying town, it never occurred to me that my heart might be in jeopardy again.

Harley Kerr

Prologue

—

Sixty or so men were crowded into the End of the Road Bar, the official gathering place for the male population of Temptation, Texas. Some sat slumped at tables with their backs rounded against spool-back chairs. Others straddled bar stools, their dusty, mud-caked boots hooked over the stools' lowest rungs. Those unfortunate enough to have arrived too late to claim a proper chair hitched a foot against chipped plaster and pressed their shoulders to the wall, while still others leaned back on elbows braced against the long, scarred bar.

Having made the trek into town straight from work on their respective farms and ranches, most of the men wore jeans and boots. Others sported bib overalls over soiled T-shirts. Since there wasn't a lady in sight to complain about the breach of etiquette, to a man their heads were covered, either with straw cowboy hats or monogrammed caps advertising farm equipment or feed.

Arriving late, Harley Kerr stopped just inside the door and looked around. Cody Fipes, his friend and Temptation's sheriff, sat at a table in the rear of the room. Harley slipped into the empty chair Cody had saved for him and was rewarded with a beer shoved his way. With a nod of thanks, he one-knuckled his sweat-stained hat to the back of his head and closed a hand around the cold brew.

"Was beginning to wonder if you were going to make it," Cody murmured in a low voice.

"Bull got in a pasture with some heifers," Harley replied dryly. "Took me a while to convince him he didn't belong there." Hot and tired, he tipped back his head and took a long, thirst-quenching drink before setting the beer down and turning his attention to Roy Acres, Temptation's mayor.

Seated on a tall stool centered in front of the long bar, Mayor Acres resembled a fly-fattened frog. His face flushed with the effort, he raised his voice a level higher to be heard over the scrape of chairs and the buzz of conversation as he called the meeting to order. The topic for the night's meeting? Temptation's quickly disintegrating population and the closing of local businesses.

Heads wagged regrettably as Mayor Acres read through the list of businesses that had closed in the past year. Lips pursed as Acres reviewed a survey taken at the local high school that revealed only seventeen percent of the students registered there intended to remain in Temptation after graduation.

Usually filled with raucous laughter and loud country music, the End of the Road was as quiet as a church on Saturday night as its occupants absorbed the depressing news about the town where they'd spent their entire lives. If something wasn't done and done fast, Temptation, like so many other rural communities, would soon be nothing but a ghost town.

Few understood this better than Harley Kerr and Cody Fipes. They'd spent a lot of time over the past few years cussing and discussing Temptation's slow decline. But unlike Harley, Cody had come up with a plan. Not one that Harley totally supported, but he figured at least it was a start.

With a tense glance at Harley, Cody stood and dragged off his hat. "Roy," he said, nervously tapping his hat against his knee, "I think I might have a solution to Temptation's problem."

"Well, speak up, then," Mayor Acres grumped impatiently. "That's why we're here."

Cody hauled in a steadying breath, not at all sure how his idea would be accepted. "What we need to do," he said slowly, "is to advertise for women."

Somewhere in the crowded room the legs of a chair hit the floor with a loud thump, and one man, caught in midswallow during Cody's brief recitation, spewed beer. Across the room someone shouted, "Hell. If you're horny, Cody, why don't you just drive up to Austin and pick yourself up a whore for the night?" The comment was met with hoots and hollers and a general round of back slapping.

Cody frowned. He hadn't expected anybody to jump on his idea, at least not at first, but he sure as heck hadn't expected to be made a fool of.

"That's not what I had in mind," he said dryly. "It doesn't take somebody with a college degree to figure out that if you want to grow a town, you need women to do it. As far as I know," he added, narrowing an eye at the man who'd told him to find himself a whore, "men haven't figured out how to reproduce on their own just yet."

He shifted, drawing his hat between his hands. "What we need to do is take a look at the businesses we've lost, assess what businesses or professionals we'll need in the future and advertise for women to move here and fill those needs."

At the word "need," someone snickered and Cody shot him a look that would peel paint off a barn. Sorry he'd even bothered to share his idea for saving Temptation, Cody rammed his Stetson back on his head. "That's all I've got to say," he muttered, then sat down.

The laughter continued and Cody's face turned redder and redder until Harley felt compelled to come to his friend's defense. With a sigh, he pushed to his feet. "You boys can laugh all you want, but I haven't heard a one of you come up with a better idea. Personally I don't give a double-damn whether any women move here or not." He waited a beat, then added, "But Cody's right when he says it'll take women to grow our town." He clapped a hand on Cody's shoulder in a show of support. "I, for one, stand behind him on this plan of his to advertise for women, and I hope all of you will do the same."

What no one in the room realized was that the reporter from the county newspaper was busily scrawling notes on a steno pad, recording Cody Fipes's plan to save Temptation right along with Harley Kerr's endorsement of the plan. When the weekly issue was delivered to its subscribers on Wednesday, the entire county would read about the meeting in the small town of Temptation, Texas, whose population had dwindled to a depressing 978, and Cody Fipes's suggestion for how to save it. By Thursday, the AP service would have picked up the story and carried it nationwide.

By Friday afternoon, news trucks and vans would line the narrow main street that marked the town of Temptation, their cameras rolling, hoping to capitalize on this story of the town who hoped to save itself by advertising for women.

Within forty-eight hours, single women from all fifty states would be gossiping—and maybe dreaming a little—about the small Texas town of Temptation where the men outnumbered the women eight to one.

One

Houston, Texas

A television sat on the apartment's breakfast bar, its volume muted, while a suited anchorman on the screen droned out the six-o'clock news. Across the narrow dining room, Mary Claire Reynolds sat at her kitchen table, cradling her sleeping eight-year-old son, Jimmy, against her breasts. Her chin rested on top of his head while hot guilty tears streaked down her cheeks and dripped onto the boy's red hair, the same unique shade as her own.

With Jimmy sitting in profile on his mother's lap, his bruised cheek and split lip were visible to the two women sitting on the opposite side of the table. They had arrived as soon as they'd heard the news of the boy being attacked, offering, as they had so many times in the past, support and comfort.

Leighanna exchanged a concerned look with Reggie, then leaned across the table to lay a comforting hand on Mary Claire's arm. "It's not your fault," she murmured softly. "You mustn't blame yourself."

Mary Claire caught her lower lip between her teeth, trying to hold back the strangled sob that burned in her throat, and tightened her arms around Jimmy. "It is," she said, unable to stop the hot angry tears that streaked down her face. "If I'd been home, this never would have happened." She cupped a hand on her son's tousled hair as if at this late date she could protect him from the fists of the gang of boys who'd attacked him. Her hand inadvertently touched the bruise on his cheek, and he roused and tried to pull from her arms. She hugged him tighter, rocking slowly back and forth, murmuring to him to soothe him back into a restful sleep.

When he had settled again, she pressed her lips to his head. "I never should've divorced Pete," she murmured with regret. "I should've listened to my mother and simply looked the other way when he strayed."

Reggie straightened, a look of shock on her face. "Mary Claire, you don't mean that!"

"I do mean it," she said fiercely. "If I'd stayed, I wouldn't have been working. I'd have been at home with my children where I belong."

"You were miserable married to Pete Reynolds," Reggie reminded her. "He was a two-timing snake."

Mary Claire lifted her tearstained face. "But we were safe. I'd gladly sacrifice my pride for my children's safety."

"What about the children's happiness?" Reggie asked. "Would you sacrifice that, as well?"

Mary Claire closed her eyes against the painful reminder.

"It's true, isn't it?" Reggie persisted. "The kids are happier now than they were when you and Pete were married. He never spent time with them. He was always too consumed with his job and chasing skirts. And when he was home, all the two of you did was fight."

"But my children were safe," Mary Claire insisted. "And I was at home with them to see that they stayed that way." She pressed her lips to the top of Jimmy's head again, then propped her chin there and turned her teary gaze on the television screen. Suddenly she stiffened, her eyes widening. "Leighanna! Quick!" she cried. "Turn up the volume on the television!"

Startled, Leighanna twisted in her chair and stretched to adjust the volume. On the screen a reporter stood in front of a sign that read Temptation, Texas, Population 978.

"Temptation? Isn't that where your aunt Harriet lived?" Leighanna asked in surprise. Mary Claire nodded but quickly shushed Leighanna with a wave of her hand, her gaze riveted on the screen.

"...and while other small rural towns around the state and around the country are slowly losing their residents to the economic pull of larger cities, Temptation, Texas, has devised a plan to save their town." The camera panned, taking in the sleepy community of Temptation.

Mary Claire felt her throat tighten at the sight of the town, remembering the lazy summers she'd spent there visiting her aunt Harriet. Things hadn't changed much through the years. Temptation still looked like a Norman Rockwell painting.

An American flag still flew above the roof of Carter's Mercantile, which served double duty as the town's post office and only grocery store. A red-and-white-striped pole turned slowly in front of the barbershop while a dog napped on the sidewalk in front of the open door. The only movement that broke the solitude came in the form of a dust-covered pickup truck as it chugged down the street.

"That's it," Mary Claire whispered. The tears were gone and her eyes now glowed with newfound hope. "Temptation. We'll move to Temptation."

Leighanna turned to stare at her friend. "Temptation?" she repeated in disbelief.

"Yes, Temptation," Mary Claire repeated firmly.

"Do you know anyone there?"

Mary Claire shook her head. "Just Uncle Bert and Aunt Harriet. But of course they're gone now."

"Oh, Mary Claire," Leighanna cried, "you can't just up and move somewhere where you don't know a living soul! Temptation's a small town. Why, there are more people living in a city block of Houston than live in that entire community."

"Exactly."

"But where will you live?" Leighanna asked, trying to keep the growing panic from her voice. "Where will you work? The reporter said the economy is drying up."

Mary Claire kept her gaze on the screen. "I have my aunt Harriet's house. There's a renter living there now, but I'll just tell him he has to move. As for work, I'll find something."

Knowing she was no match for Mary Claire's stubbornness once she set her mind on something, Leighanna turned to Reggie for help. Of the two, Reggie was the more sensible and the only one whose stubbornness equaled Mary Claire's. "Reggie, please," she begged, "see if you can talk some sense into her." When Reggie continued to stare at the screen, Leighanna gave her friend's shoulder an impatient shove. "Reggie! Help me out here!"

As if waking from a dream, Reggie turned to look at Leighanna. "What?"

Leighanna let out a huff of breath. "For God's sake, Reggie! Mary Claire says she's moving to Temptation. You've got to try to talk some sense into her! She won't listen to me. You heard the reporter. There's nothing there! The economy has all but dried up."

Slowly Reggie turned to look at Mary Claire. "You want to move to Temptation?" she asked, her face and voice completely stripped of emotion.

"Yes. If I have to take in laundry to support myself and my children, I'll do it. Anything to get us out of Houston and to a safe place."

Though she would have chosen anywhere else in the world for her friend to move, Reggie, unlike Leighanna, understood Mary Claire's need to put as much distance as possible between herself and bad memories. She leaned over to cover Mary Claire's hand with her own. "Then go," she said, giving her friend's hand a hard squeeze. "And know that if you ever need anything, whether it's a shoulder to cry on or a loan to get you by until you've found a way to support yourself, all you have to do is call."

Shocked, Leighanna nearly fell out of her chair.

Mary Claire curled her fingers around Reggie's hand and squeezed back, tears budding in her eyes. "Thank you, Reggie." She shifted her gaze to Leighanna, needing and wanting her approval, as well.

Leighanna hesitated only slightly before shifting to add her hand to the two already joined. "Personally I think you're crazy," she muttered. "But, like Reggie, I'm here if you need me."

Temptation, Texas

Harley threw the last feed sack onto the back of his truck, then stripped off his gloves and tucked them into the back pocket of his jeans. Dragging his forearm across his brow, he narrowed an eye at the June sun blazing overhead. It had to be a hundred degrees in the shade and it wasn't even noon. With a sigh, he caught the shoulder seams of his shirt between thick callused fingers and lifted in an attempt to peel the sweat-soaked fabric off his back. The day was going to be a scorcher, and although he'd been at it since well before six, his work was long from being completed. He still had the feed to unload once he reached his ranch and calves to move from one pasture to another.

On another sigh, he reached for the tailgate and started to lift, but stopped when he heard a whimpering sound coming from somewhere behind him. He turned slowly and let the tailgate fall back open when he saw a little girl, no more than five years old, limp-

ing barefoot and sniffling down the sidewalk toward
him. He didn't recognize her, but that didn't surprise
him. Ever since his old buddy, Cody Fipes, had pro-
posed that Temptation advertise for women, the town
had been overrun with strangers. He looked left and
right but didn't see another soul in sight to help the
child.

In the way of small-town chivalry, he hopped up
the step that led to the feed store and met her on the
sidewalk, prepared to offer a helping hand. "Hey,
there, sweetheart," he said, dropping to one knee in
front of her. "What's wrong?"

She hiccuped once, then lifted her face, tears dripping off her chin. "I got a sticker in my foot," she
sobbed.

"Well, here, let's have a look-see," Harley said
gently.

She laid her hand on his sleeve for balance, her
touch as light as a butterfly, then lifted her knee.
Though he strained, Harley's size prevented him from
being able to stoop over far enough to see the bottom
of her foot. Needing a better vantage point, he caught
her up under the arms and carried her toward his
pickup. "Let's set you up here, sweetheart, so I can
have a better look." He plopped her down on the
tailgate and squatted down in front of her, lifting her
foot. And there it was, tucked into the tender arch of
her foot, a green-and-yellow sticker as big as a tick.

He frowned, knowing it was going to hurt like hell
when he pulled the sticker out. "Can you count to
three?" he asked.

She sniffled, dragging a hand beneath her nose. "I
can count all the way to ten," she said proudly
through her tears.

"Well, you start counting and by the time you get to three I'll have this old sticker out of your foot."

"Okay," she said, then hiccuped again. "One... two..."

Harley gave a quick yank and the sticker came out, along with a startled cry of pain from the little girl.

At that moment and out of nowhere, about sixty pounds of clawing anger slammed into Harley's back. Startled, he stumbled to his feet, twisting around as he tried to grab ahold of what had hit him. An arm, no thicker than the branch of a willow tree, wound around his neck from behind and clung while a potato-sized fist pummeled his head. He made a grab behind him and within seconds had his hands on the shoulders and was looking into the eyes of a red-faced, redheaded boy who was fighting mad. That he was outsized didn't seem to matter to the kid. Fists flying, tennis shoes kicking at Harley's shins, he fought Harley as he screamed, "You let my sister go!"

"Now wait a minute," Harley said in frustration as he tried to keep an arm's-length hold on the kid while he angled him up against the side of his truck. "I'm not hurting your sister. I'm only—"

Before he could explain himself, Harley was hit again from behind, but this time the body that jumped him was a little heavier than the boy he'd just peeled from his back.

"What the hell—?" As he stumbled backward, a pair of legs wrapped themselves around his waist and a pair of arms locked around his neck, cutting off his air supply. A woman screamed at his ear, "Get your sister and run, Jimmy!"

Momentarily blinded by a mane of wild red hair,

Harley gasped for breath as he struggled to wedge his fingers between the arms that circled his neck and his collar. When he'd won enough space to give himself some breathing room, he glanced down to see that the boy hadn't moved an inch but was standing there bug-eyed, his mouth hanging open wide enough to catch flies, staring at Harley as if he'd grown horns.

Harley had grown something all right, but it sure as hell wasn't horns! It was on his back and who-ever—or whatever—it was, was going to turn him into a damn eunuch if she didn't quit kicking.

Having had enough of this craziness, Harley grabbed hold of the arms around his neck and twisted his body around, heaving at the same time, and sent the woman flying over his shoulder to land with a thump on the sidewalk in front of him. He followed her down, pinning her wrists on either side of her head while he straddled her. Startled green eyes stared at him through a tangle of red hair while her mouth moved ineffectively, sucking at air.

He gave her a minute to catch her breath, then re-gretted the courtesy when she started twisting and thrashing beneath him, still wanting to fight. He stilled her like he would a calf he'd just thrown to brand, squeezing his knees tighter around her chest and strengthening his hold on her wrists. He watched her face redden, her mouth open, felt her chest inflate...and knew she was fixing to let go a scream that would draw half the town.

"Don't even think it," he warned as he increased the pressure with his knees.

She clamped her mouth shut but glared at him through narrowed eyes. Her eyes suddenly shifted to something behind him and higher up. "Help me,

Sheriff!'' she cried desperately. ''This man is trying to kill me!''

Harley half turned and muttered a curse when he saw Cody standing behind him. He turned back around, dropping his chin to his chest. He knew he was going to have a hell of a time explaining all this.

Cody hunkered down beside them. ''What's going on here?'' he asked in a lazy drawl that was as much a part of him as the star he wore on his chest.

''I wasn't trying to kill her,'' Harley muttered miserably. ''I was only trying to protect myself.''

Cody bit back a smile. ''Protect yourself, huh?'' He shook his head, clearly finding it hard not to laugh as he looked at the slip of a woman Harley held pinned to the sidewalk. ''Maybe you'd better let her up, Harley,'' Cody suggested reasonably. ''I think you're safe now.''

Harley loosened his grip on the woman's hands, shifted his weight to his feet and slowly rose, careful not to let go of her until he was clear of danger.

With Harley out of the way, Cody offered the woman a hand and helped her to her feet.

Indignant, she dusted her palms across the seat of a pair of baggy jeans before she pointed a damning finger at Harley. ''Sheriff, arrest this man,'' she demanded.

''Now wait just a damn minute,'' Harley said in growing frustration. ''I haven't committed any crime.''

The woman wheeled on the sheriff, her green eyes blazing. ''He tried to abduct my children. He—''

Harley's temper, slow to rise, suddenly boiled over. ''I didn't try to abduct anybody,'' he yelled. ''I—''

She spun, bracing her hands at her hips, thrusting

her chin at him. "Then why is my daughter in your truck and why did you have my son pinned against its side?"

Harley pressed his lips together, knowing full well how all this must look. And he'd only been trying to do a good deed. He glanced at Cody for help.

But Cody just shrugged. "Maybe you'd better explain, Harley."

Harley fought back the anger and heaved a deep breath. "I was loading feed on my truck when this little girl here," he said, gesturing to the child who still sat on his tailgate, "limped by crying. Since there wasn't anyone around to help her—" he paused long enough to shoot a damning look at the woman who continued to eye him accusingly "—I perched her up there on my tailgate to pull a sticker out of her foot. Before I knew what hit me, this boy here jumped me from the back. I'd no more than pulled him off when this crazy woman jumped me from behind, screaming for the boy to grab his sister and run."

Cody listened, pursing his lips thoughtfully. The woman, to Harley's immense pleasure, had paled and was already racing to the back of his pickup. Murmuring softly, she cupped a hand to the little girl's cheek, thumbed away a lingering tear, then tenderly tipped up her foot.

"It's okay now, Mama," the child said cheerfully. "That nice man pulled the sticker out."

At the tag "nice man," the woman's gaze shot to Harley. He drew a great deal of satisfaction in pushing a broad smile across his face as hers turned a deeper shade of red. She let her daughter's foot down slowly, then picked the child up and shifted her to one hip. She motioned her son to her side. "I'm sorry,

Sheriff," she said, trying valiantly to keep her chin up and her pride in place. "It seems there's been a mistake."

Cody looked at her askance. "You don't want me to arrest him, then?" he asked innocently.

The woman frowned at the laughter in Cody's eyes. "No. That won't be necessary."

She shifted her gaze reluctantly to Harley's. "Thank you for helping Stephie." He watched as she struggled to form the apology they both knew was his due. "And I—I'm sorry for the misunderstanding." He could see that the words had left a sour taste on her tongue, because once she'd offered them, her lips puckered up like she'd taken a bite of an unripened persimmon. She spun around and marched away, still balancing the girl on her hip and holding the boy cinched tight to her side.

Standing alongside Cody, Harley watched the three of them as they crossed the street to a minivan parked in front of Carter's Mercantile.

"Well," he said, releasing a pent-up breath, "so much for the role of Good Samaritan."

Cody chuckled and slapped his old friend on the back. "Helluva way to greet your new neighbors."

Harley cocked his head to look at Cody in puzzlement. "Neighbors?" he repeated stupidly. "What new neighbors?"

Cody nodded at the woman loading her kids into her van. "That, my friend, is the new resident of the old Beacham place."

Harley scowled, sure that Cody was pulling his leg. "You know damn good and well that J. C. Vickers leases that place and has ever since Miss Harriet passed on." Harley knew this better than anyone be-

cause he'd been trying to sublease the land surrounding the house from J.C. for more than five years. But
J.C. was a stubborn old cuss, and even though he
didn't use the land, he refused to sublease it to Harley.
Said he liked his privacy and didn't want a bunch of
bawling cows disturbing his peace and quiet.

Cody nodded sagely, trying hard not to grin. "He
did until a couple of weeks ago when Mary Claire
Reynolds, Miss Harriet's niece, gave him notice to
pack up and move out." He chuckled, obviously delighted with the stricken look on Harley's face. He
knew his townspeople's business as well as he knew
his own, and he knew how badly Harley wanted that
land.

"You might pay her a visit later on," Cody suggested, thoughtfully pulling at his chin. "I hear she's
a divorcée from Houston. She might be a bit more
reasonable than J.C. was about leasing you that land.
Probably would have more use for the money than
she would for the pastures." With a chuckle he
slapped his friend on the back. "But you leave those
kids of hers alone, you hear? I'd hate to haul you in
on kidnapping charges."

He strode off laughing, leaving Harley standing on
the sidewalk in front of the feed store looking as sick
as a dog who'd just lost a fight with a skunk.

"You did the right thing, Jimmy," Mary Claire
said as she leaned across the console to give her son
a comforting pat on the knee. "You were just trying
to protect your little sister. And you did a good job
of it, I might add."

At the praise, Jimmy's chest swelled with pride. He

cut a teasing grin at his mother. "You didn't do so bad yourself."

Mary Claire shuddered, remembering the weight and strength of the man who'd held her pinned to the ground. "He was big, wasn't he?" she asked weakly.

"Bigger than a grizzly bear and twice as mean," Jimmy confirmed, unaware of the shiver that chased down his mother's spine.

"I thought he was nice," Stephie piped in from the back seat.

Mary Claire glanced at her daughter in the rearview mirror. *Nice?* Not so that Mary Claire had noticed. She was sure she'd be sporting a bruise where her backside had hit the sidewalk when he'd tossed her over his head. But it wouldn't do to frighten her daughter. She wanted her to feel safe in their new home in Temptation. She smiled weakly at Stephie's reflection while she struggled to think of something favorable to say about the man. "It was kind of him to take the sticker out of your foot," she finally said.

"Wouldn't have had the darn thing if she'd kept her shoes on like I told her," Jimmy muttered.

Stephie swelled up in a pout. "Mama said she always ran barefoot when she played here in the summers and that it felt good to feel grass under her feet. I just wanted to see what it felt like."

"Key word is *grass*," Jimmy returned dryly. "There wasn't nothin' but weeds and stickers on that playground."

When Stephie would have continued the argument, Mary Claire interceded. "That's enough, you two." She strained to peer through the windshield against the glare of the sun. "Why don't y'all help me watch for Aunt Harriet's house?"

"What's it look like?" Jimmy asked, already scanning ahead.

"A big two-story white house set back from the road with a little white picket fence running around it."

"Is that it?" Jimmy asked, pointing ahead.

Mary Claire slowed and pulled to the shoulder. From the road, the house her son pointed to was barely visible through the snarl of twisted oaks and thick cedars that grew wild around it. If Jimmy hadn't spotted it, Mary Claire knew she would have driven right past without even noticing.

But there it was, her aunt Harriet's house, sitting behind the huge live oak with a trunk so thick that as a child she hadn't been able to wrap her arms around it. She'd spent summers climbing that tree, playing hide-and-seek with her cousins and chasing fireflies at night around the two-story frame farmhouse shadowed by the tree's massive branches.

"I believe it is," she said, her voice almost a whisper as her mind slowly registered the changes. When Aunt Harriet and Uncle Bert had been alive, the trees had been carefully pruned and the lawn carpeted with green saint augustine grass. The beds surrounding the wraparound front porch had been filled with a profusion of flowers and shrubs, her aunt Harriet's pride and joy. The place was nothing at all like it looked now.

Mary Claire made the turn onto the drive, emotion clotting in her throat, wondering what Aunt Harriet would say if she saw her home now and feeling guilty that she hadn't taken a more active role in managing her inheritance—the inheritance that had enabled her to make the move from Houston.

"You've got to be kidding," Jimmy said, his wrinkled nose pressed against the side window as the house came into full view.

Mary Claire forced a smile, pushing back her guilt and her own uncertainties as she parked the minivan beside the sagging gate of the white picket fence. "Yep! This is it. Our new home. Isn't it wonderful?"

Jimmy twisted his head around to look at her, his lip curling in disgust. "If you say so," he muttered, and kicked open his door.

A shy finger from the back seat tapped Mary Claire on the shoulder. "I think it's pretty, Mama," Stephie murmured encouragingly.

Tears burning in her eyes, Mary Claire patted the tiny hand on her shoulder as she stared at peeling paint, broken windows and five years' worth of weeds. "Thanks, Stephie." She sniffed and lifted her chin. "It'll be even prettier when we get it cleaned up. You'll see." She took a fortifying breath. "Well, let's check out the inside."

The key she carried in her purse wasn't needed, as the front door stood partially open. Hesitantly Mary Claire stepped across the threshold with her children pressed at her back. If possible, the inside of the house was worse than the outside. Trash littered the entry-hall floor, wallpaper sagged in faded strips from the wall running along the staircase, and the smell of mildew and weeks-old garbage nearly stole her breath. Silently cursing J. C. Vickers, her former tenant, for not taking better care of the place, she slowly wove her way to the kitchen.

With each step, her spirits sagged lower and her excitement in moving her children to Temptation and

the house her aunt Harriet had left her grew a little
dimmer.

It just needs a good cleaning, she told herself, and
started rolling up her sleeves.

"Okay, you two," she told her wary-eyed children.
"Go out to the van and start hauling in all the cleaning supplies we bought in town." When they'd turned
to do her bidding, she started throwing windows open.
Once she had fresh air circulating, she twisted on the
faucet at the kitchen sink and murmured a silent
prayer of thanks when a spray of clean tap water hit
the bottom of the chipped porcelain sink.

At least the well hadn't run dry.

Harley stood with his arms draped across the top
of a fence post on the back side of his land, staring
off across the acreage that separated his ranch from
the Beacham homestead while his horse grazed a few
steps away. Mentally, he assessed the repairs that
would need to be made before he could move his
livestock onto the neighboring pastures. The fence
was down in a couple of places, the barbed wire
dragged low by choking vines and overgrown vege-
tation. He'd need to add a gate between his land and
theirs, he decided, for ease in rotating the cattle from
his place to theirs. Plus, he'd need to hook up his
brush hog to his tractor to clear out the cedars that
had sprung up here and there. Maybe he'd even run
a new line of fence, he thought, cutting the large acreage into two pastures. He'd need it if cattle prices
didn't go up soon. Either way, though, he needed that
land.

Which brought to mind the new owner.

He shifted his gaze to the two-story house in the

distance where sunlight glinted off the old tin roof.
On the drive beside the house, a minivan sat parked,
its doors gaping wide. Looking like ants from this
distance, the two kids who'd caused him so much
grief in town scurried back and forth from the vehicle
to the house, loaded down with boxes.

As he watched, the kitchen door swung open, and
the Reynolds woman herself stepped out onto the narrow porch, stooped by the weight of the five-gallon
bucket she carried. Straining, she lifted and swung,
sending a spray of murky water to wet the weeds
growing beyond the porch steps. She took a step back,
hooking the handle of the empty bucket over one arm
and paused to wipe the back of her hand across her
brow. With her arm raised high like that, the knot
she'd tied in her white shirt lifted and snagged against
her breasts while her baggy jeans dipped below her
navel to ride low on her hips.

And Harley couldn't make the muscles in his throat
move enough to swallow.

He was too far away to get the full effect, but he
remembered well the feel and shape of the woman
he'd held prisoner beneath him only hours before.
Slim-hipped, full-breasted, long-limbed. He'd been
too damn mad to fully appreciate her figure at the
time, but the memory was there now to tease him.

He blew out a shaky breath. A divorcée, Cody had
said. Harley quickly shook away the distracting
thought that formed in his head. Didn't matter, he told
himself. All he wanted from her was her land. Catching the reins of his horse, he swung up into the saddle
and looked back at the Beacham place just in time to
see the screen door slam shut behind her.

He'd give her a day or two to settle in, he told

himself, then he'd pay her a call. She'd probably
jump at the chance to lease him the land. He bit back
a grin. More than likely, being a city girl, she
wouldn't have a clue to the value and he could lease
it from her for a song.

That thought kept a smile on his face as he rode
back across his land toward home.

It took more than a couple of days for Harley to
get around to calling on Mary Claire. More like two
weeks. He kept telling himself he was too busy to
bother with it, but he knew in his heart he was just
plain scared to face her again. Telling himself he
didn't have anything to feel guilty about didn't help,
because he couldn't quite shake the memory of her
lying on the ground beneath him, struggling, her eyes
wide with fear, pinned by his greater strength and
weight. A gentle man by nature, it shamed him to
think he'd handled a woman in such a rough way.

But he needed that land, he told himself as he finally made the drive to the Beacham place. And if it
meant confronting the Reynolds woman and his
shame to get it, he would. He parked alongside the
picket fence and frowned at the closed but sagging
gate. From the direction of the house came the sound
of blaring rock music. Hooking a hand on the top rail,
he avoided the broken gate and swung himself over
the short fence. He strode down the winding, weed-
choked brick walk, determined to get this business
behind him.

Harley took the three steps that led to the porch of
the Beacham home at a lope, then nearly fell right
back down them when his gaze slammed into the
backside of Mary Claire Reynolds herself. She stood

on the fourth rung of a stepladder, bent at the waist, scrubbing at the front windows. Covered by a pair of ragged-hemmed cutoffs, the cheeks of her butt did a game of now-you-see-me-now-you-don't as she moved her hips in time with the beat of the music. Legs that seemed to go on forever pressed against the ladder as she leaned toward the windows...and he couldn't help but remember the feel of those legs wrapped around his waist.

Not liking the direction of his thoughts, Harley swallowed hard, then cleared his throat. "Ms. Reynolds?" he called. When she didn't respond, he raised his voice to be heard over the blasting rock music. "Ms. Reynolds!"

Startled, she jerked at the sound of his voice, then grabbed at the top of the ladder to keep from tumbling backward. Moving quickly, Harley lunged, grabbing her at the waist and hauling her to safety.

Momentarily stunned, she could only stare up into the face of the man who held her. Blue eyes, dark complexion, thick mustache and bushy brows. It took only a moment before recognition dawned. She pushed against his chest, her green eyes snapping. "Get your hands off me!"

Embarrassed to realize that his hands still circled her waist, Harley dropped them to his sides and took a cautious step back. "Sorry. I thought you were going to fall."

"I wouldn't have if you hadn't scared the life out of me." She let out a huff, tugging her T-shirt into place, then stooped to switch off the radio that sat beneath the ladder. More a George Strait fan himself, Harley sighed with relief at the silence that followed.

"What do you want?" she asked irritably.

Harley pulled off his hat and pushed his fingers through his hair. This business meeting wasn't getting off to a very good start. "Well, ma'am, I've come to talk to you about leasing your land."

Her head shot up, an eyebrow raised appraisingly. "And what need do you have for my land?"

"I'd like to run some cattle on it, if you're of a mind to lease it."

Mary Claire wiped her hands on the back of her cutoffs, trying to gather her scattered thoughts. "I hadn't thought about leasing," she said thoughtfully.

"Were you planning on using the land yourself?"

"No," she replied slowly.

"Then perhaps you'd be willing to lease it to me." He waited a beat, then added, "Seems a waste to let the land sit idle when it could be generating income for you."

He saw the gleam of interest in her eyes before she covered it with a frown. "Who said I needed income?"

Taken aback, Harley looked at her in surprise. "Well, nobody did," he said. "Just seems foolish to let good land go unused."

Mary Claire continued to frown at him, her green eyes narrowed to suspicious slits.

Harley heaved a sigh. "I can see you're not interested. Sorry to have bothered you."

He started to turn away, but Mary Claire's voice stopped him before he'd taken a full step. "I didn't say I wasn't interested. I just hadn't considered the possibility of leasing the land before."

Harley turned back. "Then you'll lease it to me?"

Mary Claire's frown deepened. She wasn't sure she wanted to do business with this man. First impressions were important to her, and her first impression of this guy had been anything but pleasant. The bruise he had given her backside was a faded reminder of that first encounter. But money was important. She couldn't afford to pass up an opportunity to generate income, no matter what the source.

"Depends," she said, folding her arms beneath her breasts as she studied him. Deciding his offer was worth considering, she motioned for him to follow her. "I was just about to take a break, anyway, so you might as well come inside. We can discuss this over a glass of iced tea."

Hat in hand, Harley followed her into the house and down the hall to the kitchen, trying to keep his excitement in rein. It wouldn't do to let on how badly he needed her land. He looked left and right, wondering at the quiet. "Where are the kids?"

"Upstairs. It's so hot I made them rest in their rooms for a while. Not that they're resting," she added dryly. "Jimmy's probably playing Nintendo and more than likely Stephie's knee-deep in dolls."

Nodding, Harley took a seat at the table she gestured to, then watched in silence as she nabbed two glasses from the cupboards and filled them with ice. She set both on the table, then went back to the refrigerator and pulled out a pitcher of tea.

Taking the chair opposite him, she filled each glass, then picked hers up. She tipped it in a silent toast and took a long drink. Mesmerized, Harley stared at the smooth column of her throat and the slender fingers that held the glass. On a sigh she set it back on the table and leveled her gaze on his. "How much?"

Giving himself a firm mental shake, Harley blew

out a slow breath. He'd already given the price a great deal of thought and named one just short of fair.

Her eyebrows shot up at his offer. "You've got to be kidding!"

He leaned back, ready to dicker. "Well," he said lazily, "the land's in pretty bad shape. I'll have to do some clearing before I can run any cattle on it. And the fencing will need some work," he added with a regretful shake of his head. "It's down in several places." He offered her a conciliatory smile. "But don't you worry. I can take care of that," he offered as if he was doing her a favor.

"At whose expense?" she asked pointedly.

Harley frowned, then replied, "I suppose I can handle that."

Mary Claire studied him a minute, then named a new price.

This time it was Harley's eyebrows that shot up. "Why, that's highway robbery!" he exclaimed.

Mary Claire leaned back in her chair, smiling smugly. She knew nothing about the value of the land, but judging by the surprised look on his face, it seemed she had been right on target when she'd plucked the sum from thin air. She lifted her tea glass and tapped it against her bottom lip as she studied him over its rim. "You said you wanted the land," she reminded him.

"W-well, I do," Harley stammered.

"That's my best offer. If you're not interested, I'm sure someone else will pay my price."

Harley shifted uncomfortably in his chair. He knew for a fact that at least one man would be willing to pay her price. Jack Barlow. And he could just see the smug look on Barlow's face if he managed to lease the land right out from under Harley's nose.

Harley huffed, then stood, jamming on his hat. "I'll pay your price," he growled.

"And you'll do the repairs needed?" she asked sweetly.

"Yes, I'll do the damn repairs." He strode for the back door, then turned. "But I want a five-year lease," he added, pointing a finger at her nose. "Or no deal."

"And whose name do I put on the lease?" she asked, obviously not wanting him to have the last word.

"Harley Kerr," he snapped, then stepped outside and slammed the door behind him.

Two

"**W**hatcha doin'?"

Harley glanced up, then straightened when he saw the little Reynolds girl standing on the other side of the fence watching him. He lifted his arm to wipe the sweat off his brow, a smile twitching at the corner of his mouth. She was a cute little thing with a little button nose and wide innocent blue eyes sparking with curiosity. "Mending fences. What are you doing?" he asked in return.

She dug the toe of her tennis shoe in the ground dejectedly. "Nothin'. Just watchin' you." She ambled closer, careful to place her hand between the barbs on the wire as she peered up at him. "Mama said I could watch you work as long as I didn't get in your way. Am I in your way?"

He chuckled, hunkering down on one knee to put

himself at eye level with her. "Now how could you be in my way when you're on that side of the fence and I'm on this one?"

She screwed up her mouth like she had to think about that, then grinned. "So I can watch?"

"You can even help if you want."

Her eyes brightened. "I can?"

"You betcha." He stood and stretched his arms over the top wire. "Grab ahold and I'll haul you over."

Her arms laced with his and he lifted her clear of the barbed wire, then set her down at his side. He nodded toward a sack of staples on the ground at his feet. "You can hand me staples as I need them."

He stooped and picked up his hammer. As he squatted down in front of the post again, he held out a hand, palm up. "Staple, please."

Smiling proudly, she dug in the sack and dropped a staple on his palm, then watched as he positioned it over the wire. He swung the hammer, quickly burying the staple in the post in two strokes.

"Wow!" she said. "You must be pretty strong to do that."

Harley shot her a wink. "Strength helps, but a careful aim is just as important."

"Mama doesn't aim so good," she confided. "She smashed her finger a while ago." She giggled and dipped her hand into the sack again. "She said an ugly word."

Harley couldn't help chuckling at the idea of Mary Claire letting loose on a cussword. "I've said a few myself when my aim wasn't right. Hurts like hel—heck."

Obviously unaware of his slip, Stephie sifted through the nails and let out a long sigh. "Mama and Jimmy are fixing that little fence that goes around our house. I wanted to help, but they said I was too little and would just get in the way."

Harley heard the disappointment in her voice and remembered a time or two when his own daughter had suffered the frustrations of being too little to do things her brother was allowed to do. The memory made a cloud of sadness drift across his heart. "You're helping me, though," he reminded her.

"Yeah, I guess." She crossed her ankles and sank down cross-legged on the ground, pulling the sack to her lap. She dug out another staple and handed it to Harley. "Do you have any little girls?" she asked, squinting up at him.

Harley froze, his fingers fumbling with the staple he'd just pressed to the post. "One, but she's not so little anymore," he murmured. "She's sixteen."

"Does she baby-sit? Mama was saying just this morning that she was going to need to find a baby-sitter for us when she starts working."

Harley had to close his eyes against the pain. Even after ten years, it still hurt to think about his daughter and son and all that he'd missed in their lives. "I don't think so, sweetheart. She doesn't live with me. She lives in San Antonio with her mother."

"You're divorced?" she asked, cocking her head.

"Yeah. For about ten years now."

"My mama and daddy are divorced, too. My daddy lives in Houston, but Mama didn't want us living there anymore because it's so dangerous." She leaned back on her elbows and stretched her legs out, pointing the tips of her tennis shoes toward the sky while she balanced the sack of staples on her stomach. "Jimmy got beat up on his way home from school and Mama cried. She said she couldn't take it anymore, so she moved us here."

Harley wanted to ask, "What couldn't she take anymore? Houston? Jimmy getting beat up? Or living in the same city as her ex-husband?" But he decided it wouldn't be right to press the child for information. "I'd imagine that'd be tough," he said vaguely.

Stephie sighed again. "Yeah. I heard my mama's friends talking, and they said guilt is what drove Mama to move."

"Guilt?" Harley said before he could stop himself.

"Yeah. When Mama and Daddy were married, she didn't have to work and she could stay at home with us. She told her friends that if she hadn't divorced Daddy and had been at home like she was before, Jimmy wouldn't have gotten beat up."

Though Harley had his own opinions, bitter as they were, about divorce and its ramifications, he only shook his head. "Some things you just can't prevent."

Stephie pressed her lips together and nodded her agreement. "That's what Mama's friends said. But Mama wouldn't listen. So she moved us here to Aunt Harriet's house so we'll be safe." She stared off into the distance at the two-story frame house that was now her home. "Jimmy says our house should be condemned, but Mama says it'll look prettier when we get it all fixed up."

Harley followed the line of her gaze, taking in the peeling paint, the rotten boards and the choking weeds. "I'm sure it will," he murmured, but his mind wasn't on the condition of the house. He was busy replaying that scene in front of the feed store when he'd peeled the child's mother off his back—and maybe understanding a little better the reason behind Mary Claire Reynolds's attack.

"Hi, Mama! I've been helping Harley mend fences."

Mary Claire looked up and saw Stephie skipping across the overgrown lawn. She bit back a groan when she saw that Harley followed a few steps behind.

"You have?" she asked, forcing a smile for Stephie's benefit.

Stephie skipped to a stop in front of her mother. "Yeah, and he said I was the best help he'd ever had." Stephie beamed a smile at Harley over her shoulder. "Didn't you, Harley?"

He stopped behind Stephie, laying a hand on her shoulder, and grinned down at her. "Without a doubt."

He glanced Mary Claire's way just as she pushed to her feet, and he had to lock his knees to keep from falling over backward. There ought to be a law, he swore silently. A woman shouldn't be allowed to walk around half-dressed like that. Wearing the same cutoffs she'd worn the day he'd caught her washing windows, she exposed a mile of tanned shapely legs. To make matters worse, instead of the T-shirt she'd had on then, she now wore a little crop top that barely covered her stomach.

Her mane of red hair was pulled up under a baseball cap whose curved bill shaded her eyes, but he could see the distrust in their green depths as she shifted her gaze to the hand he'd rested on Stephie's shoulder. From what Stephie had told him, he supposed he could understand her wariness, but he wasn't about to move his hand. He wasn't a threat to the little girl, and the woman might as well learn that now.

He tore his gaze from hers, finding it a lot easier on his system to look at the fence than confront all that bare flesh. "Looks like you've been doing some fence mending of your own."

Mary Claire glanced at the distance she'd covered that morning and let out a weary sigh. "Three hours and less than forty feet. At this rate it'll take me a year to finish."

Harley chuckled. "Once you develop a rhythm, the work'll go faster." He glanced Jimmy's way. The boy was busy ripping off rotten boards with a crowbar. "Appears you've got some pretty good help of your own."

Mary Claire smiled proudly as she looked at her son, knowing she couldn't have accomplished half of what she'd done without his assistance. "He's that all right."

"Could you use some more muscle?" Harley asked, then wondered where the offer had come from. He certainly had enough chores at his own place without taking on Mary Claire's.

She looked at him in surprise. "Oh, I couldn't ask you to take time away from your own work to help us."

"You didn't ask. I offered." He gave Stephie's

shoulder a squeeze before he pulled his hammer from the carpenter's belt strapped low on his hips. "Me and my partner here work pretty cheap."

Without waiting for a reply, he caught Stephie by the hand, winning a smile from her, and headed down to the next section of fencing. Before Mary Claire could think of an argument, he had Jimmy toting a bundle of new pickets to him and Stephie passing him nails.

Mary Claire knew that inviting Harley to eat lunch with them was the least she could do, considering he had entertained Stephie all morning, then spent another two hours working on her fence. But knowing it and liking it were two entirely different balls of wax. For some reason, the man made her uncomfortable.

With Stephie and Jimmy upstairs washing up, she laid out cold cuts and cheeses on a platter—and kept a watchful eye on Harley as he did his own washing at the kitchen sink.

He stood, one leg cocked, one hip shot higher than the other as he lathered soap between wide tanned hands. She fought back a shudder, remembering all too well the strength encased in those hands. With his sleeves rolled to his elbows, long ropes of muscles played beneath the healthy smattering of dark hair as he rubbed the lather up one forearm and down the next.

Sunlight gleaming through the window above the sink caught the bubbles that jumped to life from his brisk rubbing and turned them into hundreds of tiny rainbows. Mesmerized by the iridescent bubbles and the sheer manliness of the act, Mary Claire watched in growing fascination as he rotated his arms beneath the water to rinse off the soap. Cupping his hands, he dipped his face low over the sink and splashed water over his face and neck, then growled liked a bear, shaking droplets from his head as he groped blindly for a towel. The feral sound sent a quiver of sensation shooting through Mary Claire's abdomen.

The cold cuts forgotten, she snagged the towel and pressed it into his hand. The thick terry cloth muffled his thanks as he dragged it down his face, across the back of his neck. He turned, but stilled, his hands locked on the ends of the towel, when he found her watching him.

Something electrical passed between them as their eyes met, something charged with so much force that it shocked every nerve in Harley's body to life.

Before he could decide whether to stand or run, Mary Claire caught the corner of the towel and wiped at a stray droplet that clung to his mustache, her nervous movements as fleeting as those of a moth at a flame. But the brush of her fingers across his lips did something to his insides, making his heart do a slow somersault while his blood warmed in his veins. It had been a long time since a woman had touched him in such a way. He'd forgotten the tenderness, the comfort rendered in so simple a gesture.

On a sigh, he closed his eyes and caught her wrist in his hand. He held her palm against his cheek, absorbing the softness of her skin against his. Slowly, the thundering of her pulse trapped beneath his fingers registered in his muddled mind. Opening his eyes, his gaze settled on lips slightly parted and eyes filled with… Was it longing? Drawn by that look, he gathered her fingers in his and pressed them to his lips. He watched as her eyes widened, then darkened to a smoldering green, and his lungs burned with the need to pull her into his arms.

"Hey! What's for lunch!" Stephie called as she skipped into the kitchen.

At the sound of Stephie's voice, Harley dropped Mary Claire's hand faster than he would a hot branding iron. He tore his gaze from hers and whirled to face the sink once again, his chest heaving as he grabbed for much-needed air. Mary Claire did her own job of covering up their actions by snatching up the platter of cold cuts. But Harley saw the tremble of her fingers on the plate's edge and knew she was just as shaken as he by what had just transpired between them.

It seemed like an eternity, but he was sure it was only seconds before Mary Claire turned to greet her daughter, a smile on her face. "We're having sandwiches, and no complaints," she warned. "It's too hot to cook."

Stephie pulled out a chair and plopped into it. "That's okay. I like sandwiches." She patted the seat of the chair next to her. "You can sit by me, Harley," she said shyly.

Harley wasn't sure how he did it, but somehow he made it to the chair without his knees buckling beneath him.

"How's your new neighbor getting along?"

Harley hunched his shoulders to his ears, already regretting the impulse to stop at the End of the Road for a beer. He didn't want to talk about Mary Claire Reynolds. In fact he'd stopped at the bar hoping to drown her image in beer. "How would I know?" he replied sourly.

Cody bit back a smile. "I thought since you'd leased that land of hers, you might've seen her around."

Harley frowned. In a town the size of Temptation, everyone knew everyone else's business, but for the life of him he couldn't figure out how that bit of news had leaked out so fast. "How'd you know I'd leased the land?"

"June, over at the bank. She said the Reynolds woman made a deposit the other day. A nice fat check written on your account. I just put two and two together and figured you'd talked her into that lease."

Harley twisted his head around just far enough to scowl at Cody. "You're a genius, Cody. A bona fide genius. It's no wonder you're the sheriff."

Cody laughed good-naturedly and pounded Harley on the back. "Did you hear that, Hank?" he called out to the man behind the bar. "Harley here thinks I'm a genius. I think that calls for a beer."

"Reason enough for me." Grinning, Hank stuck a mug under the tap and pulled the lever, then decided, what the hell, and plucked up another to fill. Business was slow in the afternoon, and it was a rare moment when he had the opportunity to share a beer with his two friends. After topping off the mugs, he hooked a finger through both handles and rounded the bar. He slid one in front of Cody before hitching a hip on the nearest stool. He lifted his mug and tapped Cody's before taking a long drink.

On a satisfied sigh, he set the mug down and leaned around Cody to peer at Harley. "Would you look at that face?" he said to Cody with a woeful shake of his head. "If I didn't know better, I'd swear the man had woman troubles."

Harley's scowl deepened and he snatched up his beer. Hank hooted and gave Cody a poke in the ribs with his elbow. "I believe the man *does* have woman troubles." Ready to give his friend a hard time, he puckered his forehead thoughtfully and pulled at his chin. "Now let's see. Who could it be?" he teased. "Widow Brown," he decided, while he tried his damnedest to keep a straight face. "She's had her eye on him for years."

The widow Brown was pushing eighty and only had about four teeth left in her head, but Cody was enjoying watching Harley squirm, so he decided to play along. "Nah," he argued. "Widow Brown gave up on Harley years ago. I heard she was flirting with Duffy Smith at bingo last Saturday night. But there is that new neighbor of his," he said, talking as if Harley weren't even there. "A divorcée by the name of Mary Claire Reynolds."

Hank let out a low whistle. "Whooee! That is one fine-looking woman. I saw her the other day over at the Mercantile." He cupped his hands out in front of his chest. "She's got boobs out to—"

Harley's mug hit the bar with a thump, sloshing beer across the scarred wood as he bolted to his feet. "If you two don't have anything better to do than sit around and gossip like a couple of old ladies," he growled, "I sure as hell do!" He scraped his hat off the bar, jammed it on his head, then dug a couple of dollars from his pocket and tossed them next to his mug. He stomped out, slamming the door behind him.

Cody chuckled as he listened to the rev of a truck engine and the spray of rocks from the parking lot out front. "Yep," he said, "I believe there is definitely something brewing between our friend Harley and Mary Claire Reynolds."

The teasing had all been in jest to Hank, and now he looked at Cody in surprise. "Harley?" At Cody's nod, Hank shook his head in disgust. "If there's any interest, it's one-sided. There isn't a man alive who has less use for women than Harley Kerr. Other than me of course," he added judiciously.

"No use for women!" Cody sputtered. "You?"

Hank grinned, then winked. "Well, maybe one use."

Shaking his head, Cody dug a hand in his jeans pocket and pulled out a bill. He slapped it down on the bar between them. "Twenty says she'll have a ring in Harley's nose and be leading him around by the end of the summer."

Though the idea of Harley, or any man for that matter, falling under a woman's spell made his skin crawl, Hank was never one to walk away from a bet, especially a sure one. He took Cody's hand and shook. "You're on." He picked up his beer again and took a slow sip as the two sat in companionable silence.

"You know, Cody," Hank said after a moment, "if you're right about Harley, you're the one to blame. If you hadn't made that damn-fool statement at the town meeting about advertising for women, that

Reynolds woman would've never moved here, and
Harley's bachelorhood wouldn't be in jeopardy."

Cody laid a consoling hand on Hank's shoulder.
"Yeah, but just think of all the business that
announcement's brought your bar."

Hank thought about that for a minute, then grinned
again. "I guess a man can take some consolation in
that."

The darkness pulled at her. That and the golden
radiance of a full moon and the promise of wishes to
be made on falling stars. With the children in bed for
the night, Mary Claire pushed through the screen door
and out onto the back porch. This was her time or, as
she liked to refer to it, her alone time.

Breathing deeply of the clean night air, she moved
down the steps, her nightgown billowing around her
ankles while a gentle breeze teased her bare legs.
Seeking her favorite spot, she settled on the worn
wooden base of the old tree swing and cinched her
fingers around the rough hemp that suspended it from
a massive branch overhead. Digging a bare toe into
the earth beneath it, she gave a shove and sent the
swing into motion.

Leaning back, she let her hair drift behind her while
the breeze played through the long tresses and ca-
ressed her cheeks. Slowly she swung, back and forth,
back and forth, letting the night and the wind work
its magic until they'd cleared the webs of worry from
her mind and relaxed her tired and aching muscles.

The decision to move to Temptation had been the
right one, she reflected on a satisfied sigh. The children were happy. She was home with them every day.

She didn't have to worry about finding day care, nor did her children have to face the threat of street gangs or any of the other dangers that lurked around every corner in Houston. The house was beginning to take shape, looking more like home every day. She'd scrubbed it from top to bottom, replaced broken windows, hung new wallpaper in the entry hall and in the bathrooms. She'd polished all the wood moldings, painted the dreary kitchen. Even her work with the picket fence was progressing. Another day or two and she'd be ready to paint it. Harley had been right about that. Once she'd developed a rhythm, the work had gone much faster.

At the thought of Harley, she dragged her feet to stop the swing's motion, stirring a cloud of dust as she remembered what had passed between them in her kitchen that afternoon. What had gotten into her? she asked herself. What had made her reach out and touch him? And why had the touch of his lips against her fingers made her yearn for the touch of those same lips on hers? If Stephie hadn't come in when she had....

Mary Claire shook her head, dispelling the thought. God, she couldn't let herself think that way! She had to remain focused. She had so much to do yet. She couldn't allow a man to get in the way of her plans. Though she had accomplished a great deal in making Aunt Harriet's house a home for them, she still had to figure out a way to support herself and her children. To this day, she wasn't sure how he'd accomplished it, but her ex-husband had managed to produce enough evidence at their divorce hearing to convince the judge that he was nearly a pauper. As a result, the judge had settled a piddling amount on him for child support, which didn't come close to meeting the children's needs. Mary Claire had her savings, but she knew that wouldn't last forever. Harley's check for the lease had helped....

Harley again, she thought on a groan, cinching her hands tighter around the rope and dropping her head back in frustration. She stared through the lace of leaves and branches at the full moon overhead, willing thoughts of him from her mind. She couldn't allow him to distract her. She had to direct all her energy, both mental and physical, toward her family's security.

Hoping to leave the thoughts of Harley behind, she pushed herself off the swing and strolled around the backyard, enjoying the cool dew on her bare feet. She stopped before the fenced area that had once been Aunt Harriet's kitchen garden. Knee-high weeds, tangled and stooped, grew where tomatoes and other vegetables had once grown. She remembered the garden from her youth, the delight in picking the lush tomatoes and shelling peas with her cousins on Aunt Harriet's porch.

Leaning over the short fence, she gathered a fistful of weeds in her hand and pulled, straining until the stubborn roots gave way. She stumbled back, caught herself, then smiled. A garden, she decided. She'd plant a garden. It was too late to plant everything Aunt Harriet had once harvested. But surely there were some seeds she could sow this late in the season.

A sound on the drive made her turn, and she watched a truck pass by the side of the house, then make a wide turn around the detached garage, its headlights cutting through the darkness. *Harley?* she wondered in dismay. What was he doing here so late? Before she could make a dash for the house to avoid him, she was trapped in the glare of headlights as the truck swung toward her. Momentarily blinded, she threw up a hand, weed and all, to protect her eyes— and belatedly remembered she was wearing only a nightgown.

The truck stopped, the engine stilled and the headlights snapped off. The cab door opened with a metallic squeak, then slammed shut. She dropped her hand and snugged both arms beneath her breasts as she waited for his approach, unaware of the dirt that sifted down the nightgown's front from the weed's roots.

His gait was slow, almost lazy, as he crossed to her. The hat that seemed his constant companion shadowed his face.

"Sorry," he said, his husky voice skittering over her raw nerves. "I didn't mean to startle you." He pushed back his hat, and moonlight sharpened features that were already too familiar to her. He nodded at the arms she'd folded beneath her breasts. "A little late in the evening to be doing gardening, isn't it?"

Mary Claire looked down and was surprised to see that she was still clutching the weed. Tossing it aside in embarrassment, she brushed furiously at the dirt that clung to her nightgown. "I wasn't weeding," she replied irritably and glanced back up at him. At his lifted brow, she heaved a frustrated breath. "Well, I wasn't. I was just checking the condition of the garden plot and wondering if it's too late to plant this year."

He lifted a shoulder in a shrug. "Might have trouble with tomatoes because of the heat and all, but you could probably still plant some beans and peas. Maybe even a few varieties of lettuce, if you've a mind."

He crossed to the fence and looked over, bracing his wide hands on the top of the fence as he studied the snarl of weeds. "You'll have a hard time clearing this out by hand, though. You'll need a tiller to bust up all these weeds and turn 'em under." He cocked his head to look at her over his shoulder. "Have you got one?"

Mary Claire felt heat flame in her cheeks, feeling foolish for not having thought of that herself. "No, I don't."

He nodded thoughtfully as he turned his attention back to the garden plot. "You could probably rent one from the feed store in town. They keep a few on hand."

"Thanks. I'll keep that in mind," she replied dryly. When he didn't seem to be in a hurry to leave, Mary Claire's temper snapped. "What are you doing here, anyway? This *is* private property, you know."

Harley pushed away from the fence. "Yeah, I know. But when I left today I was in kind of a hurry—" He stopped midturn when his gaze landed on Mary Claire, reminded all over again why he'd been in such a rush to get away that afternoon and why he'd waited until the cover of night before returning.

The gown she wore, though long, was paper thin and did a pitiful job of concealing what was beneath. The moon, hanging in the sky like a ball of molten gold behind her, shot a beam right through the fabric, silhouetting her figure and making him painfully aware of her full breasts, narrow waist and the seductive curve of her hips. A body made for loving.

Unnerved, he glanced away, nodding toward the barbed-wire fence not twenty feet away. "I left my toolbox over there by the fence where I was working this morning. Thought I better get it before someone decided to claim it as their own."

Mary Claire lifted her chin. "I assure you," she replied indignantly, "that if we'd found it, we would've returned it. We don't keep what's not ours."

"Ah, hell," Harley mumbled, knowing by the tone of her voice that he'd insulted her. "I didn't mean to imply that I thought you or your kids would steal it."

"Well, what did you mean?"

"I…" He shook his head, keeping his gaze on the fence, knowing he didn't dare look her way again. His system was already on overload from the glimpse he'd had before. "Hell, I don't know what I meant. I just wanted to get my damn toolbox."

"And this couldn't have waited until morning?"

Without thinking he whipped his head around to glare at her. "Well, sure it could! But if I'd waited till morning, there was the chance of bumping into you."

Her sharp intake of breath made her breasts jut beneath the thin fabric…and he knew he'd made a mistake. He should've never looked her way again. It was a vivid reminder of what he'd tried all day to forget.

"Hellfire, Mary Claire!" he growled, trying to hold on to his temper. "Didn't you feel what passed between us today?'' He didn't wait for an answer. He didn't need one. He knew she'd felt the same thing as him. He waved a hand at her. ''And just look at you. Prissing around wearing nothing but your nightgown, looking like sin incarnate. I'm a man, with a man's needs and desires, and a man can only take so much.''

Mary Claire all but shook with fury. How dared he insinuate she was flaunting herself! She took two slow steps toward him, fisting her hands at her sides to keep from taking a swing at him. ''You're forgetting one thing,'' she grated out. ''I didn't invite you here. Not now and not this morning. And if I want to run naked in my backyard, that's my right. It's *my* backyard.''

They were almost nose to nose now, close enough that Harley could see the glint of fury in those green eyes, see the tremble of her flesh beneath the sheer nightgown, feel the heat of her anger in the narrow space that separated them. Her nearness brought something else, too. A whiff of something flowery and sweet and utterly feminine.

She lifted a hand and poked a finger at his chest. ''And another thing—''

But she never got a chance to finish the threat. Harley grabbed the finger that poked at him and used it to haul her against his chest. Before she could stop him, he crushed her mouth with his.

He felt her tense, felt her hands pushing furiously at his chest and knew he should let her go, but he couldn't have stopped even if he'd wanted to.

The woman had haunted his every step since the moment he'd first met her. Calm, she was beautiful.

Angry, with that red hair blowing across her face, dressed in nothing but her nightgown, she was irresistible. The thought of touching her again, of tasting her, had driven him to this madness. The act itself stripped him of what control he'd managed to maintain.

Knotting his fingers in her hair, he tipped her head farther back and deepened the kiss. At some point, he couldn't say when, her body grew soft against his. Her lips parted in silent invitation and on a groan he slipped his tongue inside. She tensed again at the invasion, then slowly, muscle by muscle, relaxed as his hands moved across her back.

Their tongues touched, danced, and impatiently she tugged her hands from between their bodies to loop them around his neck, drawing him closer still, her breasts pliant and soft against the wall of his chest, her heart beating in a thudding rhythm with his.

Harley had never wanted a woman more. Never like this. More than his next breath, he wanted to pull her to the ground and make love to her with nothing but the sweet smell of crushed grass beneath them and a full moon above them to guide his hands.

But he'd learned the hard way that women could be dangerous, capable of ripping a man's heart straight out of his chest. Knowing this, he tore his mouth from hers and stumbled from her embrace. "I'm sorry," he gasped. "I shouldn't have done that. I—I promise it won't happen again."

Catching her swollen lower lip between her teeth, Mary Claire crossed her arms protectively beneath her breasts and stared at him. "No, you shouldn't have," she said through trembling lips, not sure whether the anger that burned through her was because he'd kissed her or because he'd stopped. "But what's done is done." She inhaled deeply, gathering her emotions, as well as her pride. "And I think it's only fair to tell you that men don't hold the market on needs and desires. Women have a share of their own." She waited a beat, then added, "But that's something I can control. I hope that in the future you'll learn to do the same."

She wheeled and ran for the house, leaving Harley standing in the moonlight, staring after her.

Mary Claire stood in the kitchen with her back pressed to the door, her hands flattened against the thick wood. She held her breath, listening to the sound of Harley's movements through the open window above the sink. She heard the clang of metal as he tossed his toolbox into the back of his pickup, the slam of a door, then the roar of the engine as he gunned it to life. She watched the arc of headlights flash across the darkened kitchen as he swung the truck around and headed back down the drive the same way he'd come.

Only then did she dare to breathe. Her legs trembling uncontrollably, she slid to the floor, burying her face against her raised knees. What had gotten into her? she cried silently. Why had she responded to his kiss?

She sucked in a raw breath and fought back the stinging tears as the answer came. Because she was a woman with a woman's needs and desires, just as she'd told Harley, and it had been a long time since a man had touched her in such a thorough and passionate way.

She tried to bite back a sob, and when she failed, she smothered it against the thin fabric of the nightgown stretched across her knees. She'd tasted in him the same hunger, the same loneliness that haunted her every night when she crawled into bed alone. She tried to find a rational explanation for her actions and decided it was only natural that she'd fall so easily into the warmth of his embrace. She'd been alone for so long, even before she'd divorced Pete, that she was starved for a man's affection.

But it was more than that, she knew. She'd kissed other men since her divorce, and not one of them had evoked the response Harley had. If he hadn't broken away when he had...

A shiver chased down her spine and she gave herself a shake. No, she wouldn't let herself think about what might have happened. She couldn't. She was a mother, the sole provider for her children. She'd relied on a man once before and been totally dependent on him. She'd struggled long and hard to win her independence, and she wouldn't sacrifice it now for something as fleeting as sexual attraction.

Three

Mary Claire sent a warning look to Jimmy, who was already elbow deep in the cookie jar at Carter's Mercantile. "Just one," she reminded him firmly.

Ruth Martin, the proprietor of Carter's Mercantile and postmistress of Temptation, clucked her tongue at Mary Claire as she bagged her purchases. "Oh, let him have a couple." She leaned over the counter to ruffle Jimmy's hair. "Boys this age are nothin' but hollow legs and bottomless pits."

Even though Mrs. Martin had given him permission, Jimmy continued to look at his mother, knowing he had to wait for her consent. "Oh, all right," Mary Claire finally said. "But just two. You don't want to ruin your lunch."

Grinning, Jimmy snagged two, then passed another two to his sister.

"And what do you say?" Mary Claire reminded them both.

"Thank you," they mumbled around mouthfuls of chocolate-chip cookies.

Mary Claire shook her head, laughing. "You'll spoil them, Mrs. Martin."

"Oh, it don't hurt none to give a child a sweet now and then." She bagged the last of Mary Claire's groceries and pushed the sacks across the counter, then leaned conversationally against its edge. "Heard Harley Kerr leased that land from you."

Unaccustomed to her business being public knowledge, Mary Claire self-consciously passed a bag to Jimmy. "Yes, ma'am, he did."

"Glad to hear it. We'll all rest easier knowing he'll be around to keep an eye on you folks."

Mary Claire wasn't so sure *she'd* rest easier. After the episode the night before, she was already questioning her judgment in leasing the land to Harley. "I suppose," she responded vaguely.

Mrs. Martin glanced to see if the children were listening, then leaned farther across the counter and whispered, "A woman alone can't be too careful, you know. Why, someone broke into Virgie Scarborough's house while she was sleeping and stole her mother's silver right out from under her very nose."

Mary Claire's eyes widened in alarm. "Oh, my word! When?"

Mrs. Martin nodded, pleased that she had Mary Claire's attention. "Three years ago this month."

Mary Claire had to swallow a laugh. A burglary like that happened about every three seconds in Houston, but she supposed in a town the size of Temptation with its almost nonexistent crime rate, a three-year-old burglary would still be news. "We'll keep that in mind," she said.

Remembering the flier she had in her purse, Mary Claire pulled it out. "Would you mind if I hung an advertisement in your window?"

Mrs. Martin held out her hand. "Let's have a look." She dragged a pair of reading glasses from the top of her head and pushed them onto her nose. "M. C. Reynolds Bookkeeping Service," she read, then glanced up at Mary Claire, a smile spreading on her wrinkled face. "So you're going into business for yourself, are you?"

"Yes. Or at least I hope to. Do you mind if I hang the flier in your window?"

"I'll hang it myself," Mrs. Martin assured her. She studied the flier a minute, then pulled off her glasses and pushed them back onto the top of her head. "You might want to run an ad in the county newspaper. It's just a weekly, but the classifieds are reasonable enough and nearly everyone in a forty-mile radius subscribes."

Pleased to know this, Mary Claire extended her hand. "Thank you, Mrs. Martin. I'll certainly give it a try."

"You're more than welcome. And you and your young'uns come back to see me real soon, you hear?" she called as they left.

After parking the van by the garage, Mary Claire handed each of her children a bag of groceries, then tucked one under her arm and slammed the van door with her hip. She was halfway to the house before

she realized that something was different. She stopped
and looked around, her eyes widening when her gaze
landed on the garden. Without a thought for the contents of the sack she carried, she dropped it and ran.
Cinching her hands tightly on the garden gate, she
stared in disbelief. The weeds were gone, the earth
turned and plowed into six neat rows.

She stepped back, placing a hand over her heart to
calm its wild racing. Harley, she thought. It couldn't
have been anyone else. But why had he tilled her
garden?

She took another step back, then another, unable to
believe he'd done something so unbelievably kind for
her—especially after the words they'd exchanged the
night before.

Mary Claire slipped the last dish onto the drain
board, then rested her stomach against the counter's
edge and stretched to look out the kitchen window.
She'd given up several luxuries when she'd left Houston to make her home in Temptation. A dishwasher,
a garbage disposal, central air-conditioning, to name
but a few. But the pleasure of looking out her kitchen
window to wide-open spaces and listening to the birds
chirping merrily in the trees that shaded the backyard
more than made up for the lack of conveniences.

She relaxed a moment and let her mind wander,
simply enjoying the view. The changes in the scenery
just beyond the open window were dramatic. She and
the children had cleaned up the yard, tossing out all
the rubble J. C. Vickers had left behind. At the moment a lawn sprinkler spun slowly, soaking in the
fertilizer she'd spread that morning on the freshly

mowed grass. Within a few weeks the grass would be green again and the weeds would begin to die out. By summer's end, if she had her way, the lawn would look the same as it had when Uncle Bert and Aunt Harriet had been alive.

She sighed, letting her gaze travel to the back of the property. The clearing Harley had done along the back fence line had opened up the view to the pastures beyond. She now had an unobstructed view of the acreage that stretched as far as the eye could see. Lost in thought, she almost jumped out of her skin when the nose of a tractor popped up over the rise.

With a huff of breath at her own skittishness, she watched as the tractor cleared the hill and came fully into view. It was a huge machine and pulled some sort of mower behind it, its power evident in the wide swath it cut through the occasional small cedar and waist-high weeds that covered the pasture.

She squinted until she could make out the shape of the man inside the tractor's enclosed cab. Broad shoulders and the ever-present hat identified the driver. She let out a sigh. Harley. As much as she hated the thought of talking to him again, she knew she had to thank him for tilling her garden. Putting it off certainly wouldn't make the task any easier.

Snatching her baseball cap from the kitchen counter, she pushed open the screen door. As it slapped into place behind her, she paused to stuff her hair under the hat. With her shoulders squared in determination, she strode for the fence.

Harley saw Mary Claire marching across the backyard and muttered a curse when it became obvious she was headed straight for him. At the fence line she stopped, gave him a tight wave, motioning for him to join her, then folded her arms beneath her breasts and waited. He could tell by the look on her face that she wasn't happy to see him, but then, he wasn't too happy to see her, either. A guilty conscience was a hard thing for a man to live with, and even worse when confronted with the source of that guilt.

He drove on, the enclosed cab of the tractor muffling the roar of the engine and the loud whir of the brush hog he pulled. He was convinced she was going to tell him she'd changed her mind about leasing him the land. After the way he'd treated her the night before, he supposed he could understand such a decision. But dang it! He couldn't help it if the woman did things to his sanity that defied reason. He'd said he was sorry and meant to stand by his promise that it would never happen again.

At the fence he brought the tractor to a stop and went through the motions of shutting off first the mower, then the tractor, stalling for time. Silence rang in his ears as he pushed open the cab door and swung to the ground. He pushed back his hat and strolled toward her. "Afternoon, Mary Claire," he said, hoping to keep his voice neutral.

"Good afternoon, Harley." She waited until he reached the fence and stood opposite her. She nodded toward the path he'd cut behind him. "I see you're already clearing the land."

Harley shoved his hands in his jeans pockets, prepared to argue the legalities of the lease he'd signed if needed. "Yes, ma'am. I told you I planned to."

"Yes, you did." She stood a moment, her gaze riveted on the land behind him. Then she dropped her gaze to the ground at her feet. "I didn't intend for you to till my garden. But I…well, I appreciate your doing it," she mumbled.

It was a backhanded thank-you at best, but Harley hadn't done the work to reap any gratitude from Mary Claire Reynolds. He'd tilled the garden to alleviate his own guilt for his actions the night before. Sure that she had more to say, like she'd changed her mind about leasing him the land, he waited for the next shoe to fall.

When she continued to stare at the ground, digging the toe of her shoe into the freshly mown grass, he asked uncertainly, "Is that all you wanted?"

Her head came up, her gaze bumping his, and he felt that same tear through his system that looking at her always caused him. She frowned and looked away again, unable—or unwilling—to look him in the eye. "Yeah," she said, her gaze fixed on something over his shoulder. "That's it."

"Hi, Harley!"

Harley glanced behind Mary Claire to see Stephie skipping across the grass toward them. In spite of himself, a grin spread across his face. The kid was just too dang cute. "Hey, shortcake. What are you up to?"

Mary Claire turned, too, frowning at her daughter. "She's supposed to be resting."

Stephie cocked her head, charming her mother with a bright smile. "But I'm all rested up and I saw Harley through my window." She easily sidestepped her mother and moved closer to the fence. Grinning up at Harley, she turned all her charm on him. "Is that your tractor?"

"Yeah, it is."

"Will you take me for a ride?"

Mary Claire's mouth dropped open. "Stephanie Reynolds! I'm sure Harley has better things to do than ride you around on his tractor."

Knowing he was already on Mary Claire's bad side, but not wanting to disappoint Stephie, Harley sought to keep the peace. "I don't mind, as long as it's okay with you. She can ride along while I mow the pasture."

Mary Claire shifted her gaze from her daughter's hopeful face to the huge tractor that loomed behind Harley. "Are you sure it's safe?" she asked hesitantly, worrying her lip.

"Absolutely."

"And she won't be in your way?"

"Positive." He leaned across the fence and Stephie laced her arms over his, laughing as he lifted her clear of the fence, then swung her up into his arms.

She tossed an arm across his broad shoulders and pressed a kiss to his cheek—and Harley lost a little bit more of his heart to her. She leaned back in the crook of his arm. "Can I drive?"

"Stephie!" Mary Claire exclaimed, already bolting for the fence, ready to snatch her daughter back across to safety.

Harley chuckled, then shot Mary Claire a wink, stopping her. "Have you ever driven a tractor before?" he asked, cocking his head to look at Stephie.

Her hopeful expression dimmed somewhat. "No," she admitted reluctantly.

He hefted her up into the cab, then climbed onto the tall step. "Well, I guess you'll just have to sit on my lap, then, until you learn all the controls.'' He closed the cab door behind them, cutting off Stephie's reply and leaving Mary Claire standing at the fence, wringing her hands.

She watched as he settled Stephie on his lap. Her daughter—her baby, for God's sake!—looked so small against his big frame and even smaller compared to the massive tractor. Mary Claire felt her stomach turn over, and she had the strongest urge to yank Stephie off the tractor before it was too late. But then the engine roared to life and a grin split Stephie's face as she leaned forward, waving wildly at Mary Claire through the windshield. Sitting back, she wrapped her fingers around the huge steering wheel.

Harley's mouth moved, but Mary Claire couldn't hear his words over the whir of the mower. He tipped a finger to his hat, then placed his hands on the wheel next to Stephie's. Turning it, he made a tight circle, his head cocked over his shoulder to see the ground behind him until he'd positioned the mower alongside the swath he'd already cut. The tires straightened and the tractor moved off with a lurch, Harley's wide shoulders blocking Mary Claire's view of her daughter.

She'd intended to tackle the fireplace in the living room that afternoon and give it a good cleaning, but with Stephie out on the tractor with Harley, Mary Claire couldn't bring herself to leave the backyard. Needing something to occupy her hands, as well as her mind, she gathered the packets of vegetable seeds she'd impulsively picked up in town that morning.

After selecting a trowel from the tools in the shed, she headed for the garden.

Kneeling, she flipped over the first packet of seeds and read the directions on the back. "'Plant the seeds six inches apart and about two inches deep,'" she read aloud. Sounded easy enough. With a shrug, she tossed down the packet and picked up her trowel. She stabbed it into the freshly turned soil, then glanced across the field just in time to see the tractor's nose dip over the rise. Her stomach did a somersault as she watched the huge machine that carried her daughter disappear from sight. *He said it was safe*, she reminded herself.

She made herself lay aside the trowel and pick up the packet of seeds, though she would rather have run to the fence and waited for the tractor's return. Knowing it was foolish to worry, she forced her attention to her work. Even so, her hands trembled slightly as she ripped open the packet and shook out a seed. She dropped it into the shallow hole she'd dug, then scraped the dirt back over the hole, covering the seed, grateful that she could hear the rumble of the tractor even if she couldn't see it.

She worked for hours, alternately digging holes and planting seeds, always keeping a watchful eye on the tractor's slow progress through the distant field. Each time it disappeared over the rise, she held her breath until it reappeared, its nose pointed toward her. She moved from row to row, planting beans and peas and peppers and myriad other vegetables she planned to harvest later in the summer, and silently prayed her children would at least sample each. Their tastes were narrow, as most children's were, but she could already see their table heaped high with black-eyed peas, green beans and fried okra, and she mentally calculated the savings on her grocery budget.

When the planting was complete and Harley still hadn't returned with her daughter, she unhooked the hose from the sprinkler and dragged it to the garden plot to water down the narrow rows and give the seeds a better chance of germination. She was standing with her thumb squeezed over the end of the hose, shooting a spray of water to the farthest corner when she heard the tractor approach the fence. Dropping the hose, she ran and turned off the faucet. By the time she reached the fence, Harley was on the ground and holding his arms out for Stephie.

Stephie leapt into them, slinging an arm around Harley's shoulder as he shifted her to his hip. Her face was wreathed in a smile as she twisted to look at Mary Claire. "Did you see me, Mama? I drove the tractor!"

"I sure did, sweetheart! Did you have fun?"

"Yeah! Did you know a creek runs through our land? Harley showed me. He says its the bestest place in the world for a picnic. Can we go on a picnic, Mama? Can we, please?"

"We'll see," Mary Claire replied vaguely.

"And you know what?" Stephie continued. "Harley has a pony and he says I can ride it!"

Harley winced and cut a guilty look to Mary Claire. "I told her she could, but only if it was all right with you."

Mary Claire wasn't ready to discuss riding a horse just yet. Her nerves were only just beginning to settle now that she knew Stephie was off the tractor and safe. "We'll see, sweetheart," she replied, hedging.

"It's his daughter's pony, but she doesn't ride him anymore 'cause she lives far away."

A daughter? Mary Claire looked at Harley in surprise. She hadn't known he had a daughter.

"Can Harley eat dinner with us?" Stephie asked, catching Mary Claire totally off guard.

"Well, I—I don't know," Mary Claire stammered.

Harley heard the reluctance in her reply and gave Stephie a hug. "Thanks, shortcake, but not this time. I've still got some work to do back at my place."

"You could come over after you're finished. We don't eat until late. Isn't that right, Mama?" Stephie asked, turning to Mary Claire for verification.

Mary Claire was definitely on the spot. She didn't really cherish the idea of sharing a meal with Harley, but to refuse now after Stephie had issued the invitation would be rude. "That's right," she said on a sigh. "We don't usually eat until about seven."

"I wouldn't want to impose."

Mary Claire forced a smile, though her heart wasn't in it. "You wouldn't be. I put on a pot roast earlier today, so there's plenty."

"Well, if you're sure," he said doubtfully, knowing damn good and well Mary Claire didn't want him there, but not wanting to disappoint Stephie.

"I'm sure."

Stephie let out a whoop and squirmed until Harley lifted her over the fence and her feet hit the ground. "Where's Jimmy? I want to tell him about driving the tractor!"

Mary Claire looked lovingly down at her daughter

and smoothed her windblown hair back into place. "Where do you think? In his room playing Nintendo."

Stephie ducked under her mother's hand and shot for the house at a dead run, anxious to share her adventures. Alone with Harley, Mary Claire stood, awkwardly shifting her weight from one foot to the other, not sure what to say.

If possible, Harley seemed as uncomfortable as she was. He scraped back his hat and scratched his head. "Well, I guess I better get going. I'll see you about seven." He turned and swung back up into the cab of his tractor. The engine roared to life as he slammed the door. Mary Claire stood at the fence and watched as he maneuvered the huge piece of equipment back around and headed for home.

She shook her head and headed for the house, silently cursing Stephie for inviting the man to dinner.

Bent over the open oven door, Mary Claire called, "Come on in!"

Harley pulled open the screen and stepped inside, dragging off his hat. The scent of roasted meat and potatoes greeted him, making his mouth water. But the sight of Mary Claire stooped over the oven, the fabric of her slacks stretched tight across her rear end, dried the water in his mouth right back up.

Frowning, he cleared his throat. "Sure smells good," he said, trying to keep his gaze focused on the wall above the stove.

Mary Claire turned, her mittened hands tightly gripping the handles of the roasting pan. "Thanks. I—" But whatever she'd been about to say flew right

out of her head the instant her gaze landed on Harley.
She'd never seen him cleaned up before. He'd always
worn shirts and jeans stained with grease and sweat
and God only knew what else. Now he was dressed
in starched jeans and a crisp Western-cut shirt the
color of a robin's egg, making his blue eyes seem that
much bluer. His hair was damp and combed and
neatly parted, and she'd swear he'd even taken the
time to trim his mustache. The results were devastat-
ing.

"My," she said, releasing her breath. "Don't you
look nice."

Harley's cheeks flamed at the compliment. He
looked down at his shirtfront, then back at her. He
shrugged, self-consciously shifting the brim of his hat
through his fingers. "I had to tend a sick cow after I
got home. I figured y'all wouldn't enjoy sitting down
to dinner with me with the smell I carried."

Mary Claire couldn't help but laugh. "I'm sure
we'll all be grateful." She stepped quickly across the
kitchen and set the pan down on an insulated pad on
the counter. "Sorry," she said to him over her shoulder. "But I'm running a little late. Dinner won't be
ready for a few minutes."

Harley set his hat on the edge of the counter. "Can
I help?"

Mary Claire whirled to stare at him, shocked by the
offer. She couldn't remember Pete ever helping out
in the kitchen. He'd always considered that women's
work. And here Harley stood, this bear of a cowboy,
this man's man, ready to jump in and offer his help.
She shook her head. "No thanks. I've got it under

control. The kids are in the den watching television. If you want, you can—''

At that moment Stephie came skipping into the kitchen. "Hi, Harley!" She grabbed his hand. "Want to see my room?"

Harley looked at Mary Claire for approval. She nodded her head, then turned her gaze on Stephie, smiling. "Fine with me. But don't be too long," she warned. "Dinner will be ready in a few minutes."

Stephie dragged Harley down the hall and to the stairs, chattering like a magpie. Harley listened with only half an ear, his attention riveted on the changes the house had undergone since Mary Claire and her kids had moved in. He'd been a guest in the Beacham house several times over the years when Burt and Miss Harriet had been alive, and he'd always admired the stately old home. But his most recent memories of the place were the visits he'd made to J. C. Vickers when he'd tried to talk the old cuss into subleasing the land. Not a man who leaned toward cleanliness or housekeeping, Vickers had let the house go. As a result, it had smelled worse than Vickers himself. Harley had always kept his visits brief.

But now the house carried more pleasant scents— the aroma of the roast sitting on the kitchen counter waiting to be carved tangled with the scents of fresh paint and lemon furniture polish. As he climbed the stairs behind Stephie, he noticed the wallpaper had been changed. The pattern of tiny mauve rosebuds drew the rich tones from the mahogany banisters in a way that the muted and stained paper of before never had.

"This is Mama's room," Stephie said, stopping before the first door at the top of the stairs. "She picked this room closest to the stairs so she could stop me and Jimmy before we fell down the stairs and broke our necks if we wandered in the night."

Harley chuckled, sure that Stephie wasn't exaggerating. He'd seen that protective glint in Mary Claire's eye when he'd lifted Stephie onto the tractor and knew damn good and well the woman had worried herself sick the entire time they'd been gone. She was that kind of mother. But he didn't hold that against her. In fact, he respected her all the more for it.

He peeked into the room, feeling a little guilty for doing so. A brass bed dominated the far wall, its mattress graced with a quilt in the Wedding Ring pattern. Fluffy pillows in the same rich hues as the quilt lined the headboard. Along the wall next to the bed sat a dresser, its polished surface dotted with framed pictures of the kids. A breeze lifted the lace curtains at the windows and carried that same sweet flowery scent that seemed so much a part of Mary Claire.

It was a woman's room, a mother's room, and he felt the oddest tightening in his chest upon seeing it.

Stephie tugged on his hand. "Come on. I'll show you my room."

Reluctantly Harley followed her. At the second doorway, she stopped and withdrew her hand, then folded her arms over her chest. "This is it!" she said proudly. "Isn't it beautiful?"

Harley felt a wad of emotion rise in his throat. It *was* beautiful and so much like his own Jenny's room that he had to fight back tears. "Yeah, shortcake, it is," he murmured.

She grabbed his hand again, tugging him inside.

"These are my babies," she said, stopping beside her bed.

A covey of dolls lay propped against white eyelet pillow shams. He remembered a time when Jenny's dolls had adorned her bed. Now there was nothing but dust to greet him when he dared to peek into her old room.

Stephie picked up one of the dolls and cradled it lovingly against her chest. "This is Michelle, my favorite." She placed a warning finger to her lips. "But don't tell the others," she whispered to Harley. "I wouldn't want to hurt their feelings."

Harley crossed his fingers over his heart. "I promise."

Mary Claire's voice drifted up the stairs. "Dinner's ready," she called.

Stephie quickly placed Michelle with the others on the bed and grinned up at Harley. "Want to race?" she challenged, her eyes twinkling. Before he could answer, she shot out of the room and down the hall.

Harley stood a moment longer staring at the dolls on the bed. He wished with all his heart he'd spent more time with Jenny when she'd been Stephie's age, listening to her chatter about her dolls, making promises with her to keep.

He'd never realized the preciousness of those years until she'd been ripped from his heart and his home. He'd always thought he'd have a lifetime with her— but all he'd been given were six measly years.

Harley and Mary Claire sat in twin rockers on the front porch, rocking slowly while they watched Stephie and Jimmy chase fireflies through the darkness beneath the live oak's massive branches. The silence between them was easy, the scrape of the rockers against the wooden porch floor soothing.

"I didn't know you had a daughter," Mary Claire said softly.

The statement was unexpected, slipping out of the darkness like a thief to snatch at Harley's heart. "And a son," he replied, shifting uncomfortably in the chair.

"How old are they?"

"Jenny's sixteen now, and Tommy's nineteen next month."

"Where do they live?"

"In San Antonio with their mother."

Mary Claire glanced his way. "You're divorced?"

Harley let out a sigh. "Going on ten years."

"Do you see them often?"

"Not often enough."

Mary Claire heard the regret in his voice and responded to it. "It's hard to say who divorce is harder on, the children or the parents."

Harley frowned, his gaze fixed on the darkness beyond the porch and the sound of the children's voices. "I'd say it's probably hardest on the one who's left behind."

She heard the bitterness in his words, and though she disagreed, she kept her thoughts to herself.

An owl hooted from a distant tree, but it was Stephie's shriek that had both Mary Claire and Harley jerking their rockers to a stop in alarm. They watched Stephie run for the front porch, her hands cupped in front of her.

"I caught one! I caught one!" she cried in excitement as she stumbled up the steps.

Harley breathed a sigh of relief when he realized the child wasn't hurt. He stooped down and picked up the jar that sat on the floor between the rockers. "Well, let's put it in here, shortcake." He unscrewed the lid and held the jar steady while Stephie carefully fitted her hands over its top. The firefly dropped to the grass clippings tucked inside the jar, its tail blinking on and off like a lighthouse beacon. Harley quickly replaced the pierced lid.

Stephie took the jar and held it up, her eyes filled with wonder. "How does it do that?" she whispered.

"Oxidation," Harley explained.

A frown gathered between Stephie's brows. Harley struggled to think how to explain the process in terms she'd understand and couldn't come up with a single thing.

"Fairy dust," he finally said and eased his shoulders back against the rocker, ignoring Mary Claire's surprised look. "A fairy sprinkles magical dust on the firefly's tail, giving it a glow to light its way."

A smile spread across Stephie's face and the wrinkles at her brow disappeared. She thrust the jar back to Harley. "I'm gonna catch me another one."

She was halfway down the steps when Mary Claire's words stopped her. "Not so fast, Stephie," she ordered gently. "It's time for you to get ready for bed."

"Oh, Mama, please? Just a little while longer?"

Mary Claire remained firm. "It's already past your bedtime." She stood and cupped her hands at her mouth and called across the lawn, "Jim-my! Time to come in and get ready for bed."

Harley heard the boy's groan and knew he wasn't any happier than his sister about ending their play. Taking his cue, Harley stood. "I guess I better be heading home myself," he said, stretching.

Stephie angled up beside him, pressing her wafer-thin body against the side of his leg. "Will you read me a story before you go?" she asked, tipping her face up to peer at him as she slipped her hand into his.

At the feel of her tiny hand, Harley knew that if she'd asked him to walk on hot coals, he'd have done it without a second thought. He glanced at Mary Claire, hoping she wouldn't deny him this little bit of heaven. "I suppose I could stay long enough for that," he murmured.

Giving his hand a squeeze, Stephie released it and skipped to the front door. "I'll be quick as a minute getting my bath," she promised as the screen door slammed behind her. He listened to the patter of her bare feet as she skipped up the stairs.

Jimmy appeared out of the darkness, his cheeks flushed from the night's hunt. He dragged his feet as he climbed the porch steps. His hand on the screen door, he paused and looked back at Harley.

"If you need anybody to help you drive the tractor tomorrow, I'd be willing to help you out."

Harley heard the hopefulness in the boy's voice, and though he knew his work in the pasture was complete, he figured a few more cuts across the field wouldn't hurt. He gave the boy a nod. "About nine, then. Wait at the back fence and I'll come by for you.''

Grinning from ear to ear, Jimmy ripped open the screen door and shot through, letting out a whoop as he loped up the stairs.

Mary Claire's voice eased through the darkness behind Harley, moving like a caress of thick velvet on the back of his neck. ''You've already finished mowing the pasture, haven't you, Harley?''

He shrugged. ''Won't hurt to give it another cutting.''

Her hand touched his arm and he felt his heart jump in his chest. ''You don't have to do these things for them,'' she said softly.

He turned, but her hand remained on his arm. Silhouetted by moonlight, she looked up at him, her eyes filled with questions he didn't have answers for. The breeze caught the ends of her hair and blew it back from her face, and he had the most undeniable urge to follow the wind's movements with his fingertips. But he'd promised he wouldn't touch her again, and he intended to make good on that pledge. ''I know,'' he said, and shifted his gaze to his feet. ''But I want to.''

Mary Claire sighed and removed her hand. ''Thank you,'' she whispered.

Harley snapped his head back up. ''For what?'' he asked, confused.

''For giving my children adventures and memories they'll never forget.''

Four

Harley stood at the door to Jenny's room, his feet braced wide, his hands folded across his chest, his thumb massaging the ache in his chest. Tears, thick and hot from years of suppression, slipped down his cheeks in a slow journey to his jaw as he stared at the empty room, trying to remember the details of its contents when Jenny had still lived here.

There had been a double bed with a white eyelet cover just like Stephie's with dolls spread across its top. And posters of animals on the wall—his Jenny had always loved animals. A little table had stood catty-corner to the window, and Jenny had sat there whiling away the hours on many a rainy day by coloring pictures for her daddy from books he'd brought her from town.

When he closed his eyes, Harley could almost hear

her childish voice, squealing when he tossed her into bed at night. He would tickle her ribs until she'd beg, laughing, for him to stop. It was a ritual, a nightly one, before they settled down with a book. It was a ritual he'd almost forgotten.

He supposed it was the storybook he'd read to Stephie, that tiny slice of heaven Mary Claire had allowed him, that had made him seek out this room. Under Mary Claire's watchful eye, he'd sat on top of Stephie's bed with her narrow shoulders tucked beneath his arm. She'd hugged a doll to her chest as she studied the pictures on each page, listening while he read the story aloud, occasionally lifting her head to give him a smile.

When he'd arrived home, he had headed straight for Jenny's room, something he rarely found the courage to do. After Susan had moved out, taking the kids with her, he hadn't been able to so much as walk past his children's rooms to go to bed at night. Instead, for months he'd slept on the sofa in the den, avoiding the pain by avoiding the reminders.

He dragged a hand across his face, wiping away the tears, and turned away. He stopped at his son's room and opened the door to peer inside. Like Jenny's, Tommy's room held only the few odd pieces of furniture he'd collected after they'd moved to San Antonio—a bed, a highboy and a chair. Once, posters of Tommy's sports idols had covered every available bit of wall space, and his baseball bat and pitcher's mitt had hung from a pegged board Harley had made himself. Like everything else, Susan had taken it with her when she left, leaving nothing but shadowed reminders on the wall that something had once hung there.

With a sigh, Harley closed the door. He walked down the hall to his own room and began to strip off his clothes. Unlike the children's rooms, this room didn't haunt him. When she'd left, Susan had emptied the room they'd shared, just as she had all the other rooms in the house, taking with her every stick of furniture, every picture, pillow and knickknack they'd accumulated together over the years. He let her have it all without an argument because he wanted his kids to have the security of being surrounded by familiar things when she moved them all to San Antonio and unfamiliar turf. He didn't miss the possessions, he didn't miss his wife…but damn, he missed his kids.

Naked, he crawled into the empty bed and rolled to his back, pillowing his hands behind his head. As he stared at the ceiling, loneliness weighed like an anvil on his chest.

He knew there were those in town who attributed his solitary life to his inability to get over the desertion of his wife. But they were wrong. Though he'd loved Susan with all his heart from the time they became sweethearts in high school until the moment she told him she was leaving, he'd dealt with that pain. When she left him, anger and disillusionment had gone a long way in erasing any feelings for her that had remained. It was that same disillusionment that had kept him from seeking out another woman to take Susan's place in his bed or in his heart.

He sighed and rolled to his side, wadding one pillow under his ear and draping an arm around another to drag it to his chest. He closed his eyes. During his twelve years of marriage, he'd slept every night curled against his wife's back, spoon fashion, his arm wrapped around her waist. She'd always complained about the arrangement, saying either his arm was too heavy or it was too hot to be held so close. But he'd always found it comforting, and though he didn't miss his wife, he missed that added warmth in his bed.

Caught in that foggy mystical world of being half asleep and half awake, Harley yawned and snugged the pillow tighter against his chest—and wondered if Mary Claire Reynolds liked to cuddle when she slept. He'd be willing to bet she did. From the kiss they'd shared, he could tell she was a passionate woman, one who would enjoy intimacy rather than shun it.

The pillow he held slowly began to take on a shape and a warmth against his body. He could almost feel the soft curve of Mary Claire's narrow waist beneath the bend in his arm, the thrust of her rounded buttocks curled against his groin. As the image grew, her breasts, full and ripe, rose and fell, tickling the hairs on his arm with each rhythmic breath she drew. The scent of her, that sweet flowery fragrance he had smelled in her bedroom, drifted just beneath his nose, teasing him.

His blood warmed as the image of her built and he felt the familiar swell and ache of his manhood as it rose to life against his thigh. On a groan, he tossed the pillow away from him and bolted from the bed, fully awake. His chest heaving, his stride determined, he headed for the shower, turned the water on full force and stepped beneath the cold spray.

At nine o'clock sharp, Jimmy stood at the fence waiting, just as Harley had instructed. Beyond him,

Mary Claire and Stephie knelt in the garden, their heads tipped together, one blond, one red, their fingers buried in the freshly turned earth. At the sound of the tractor, they lifted their heads in tandem and turned Harley's way. He looked at the three of them from the advantage of the tractor's high cab with the sun haloing their expectant faces and wondered if God had sent them to him as a gift to make up for the loss of his own family…or as a punishment for some unknown deed from his past.

As he neared, Mary Claire pushed to her feet, grabbed Stephie's hand and hurried to the fence to wait beside Jimmy. She wore a smile, a tentative one at best, but it still managed to make his pulse kick into a higher gear as he swung the cab door open.

"Good morning, Harley," she called as he stepped from the tractor.

His foot hit the ground at the same moment his gaze met hers, and he nearly stumbled, recalling the image he'd drawn the night before of her curled against him in sleep. The full breasts, the narrow waist, the soft curve of her hips. All were there before him now, blatant reminders of the accuracy of his mind's drawing. Heat burned his cheeks and he mumbled a quick "Mornin', Mary Claire," and snugged his hat farther over his brow for fear she might read his lustful thoughts in his eyes.

He quickly shifted his gaze to Stephie, who was hopping from one foot to the other, impatiently waiting for him to notice her. Grinning, he stretched his arms over the fence and she leapt into them, stretching to plant a wet kiss on his cheek as he lifted her across.

"Are you gonna take me for a ride, too?" she asked hopefully, pressing back in his arms far enough to look him in the face.

Harley chuckled and tweaked her nose. "Now if you go, too, who'll stay and keep your mama company?"

Stephie dipped her chin, looking so dejected it almost broke his heart. "Yeah, I guess you're right," she murmured.

Harley gave her a hug. "You help your mother, and when I get back, maybe she'll let you come over and see the pony."

"Really?" she asked, her eyes growing wide.

"Yes, really." He gave her another quick hug, then set her back down on the other side of the fence. "You about ready to go?" he asked Jimmy.

"Yes, sir," Jimmy replied.

Suspecting the boy wouldn't want to be handled like Stephie, Harley lifted the middle wire high enough for Jimmy to scoot between it and the one below, then let it drop back into place. "If it's all right with you, Mary Claire," he said, turning to her, "I thought Jimmy and I might mow the highway frontage there in front of your house. It's been a while since the county had a crew through here."

Though she frowned at the unexpected change in plans, Mary Claire lifted a shoulder in a shrug, assuring herself that she would still be able to keep an eye on them. "I guess that would be okay."

With a nod Harley turned for the tractor where Jimmy was already scrambling up the high step. Mary

Claire's voice chased him into the cab. "Jimmy! You mind Harley and don't push any buttons unless he says you can."

Jimmy's red-haired head popped out the cab door, his face wreathed in a wide smile. "Yes, ma'am. I promise." Then he disappeared again, and the door closed behind Harley, leaving Mary Claire once again standing at the fence wringing her hands.

She became aware of what she was doing and dropped her hands to her sides in disgust. "I refuse to stand here all day and watch that silly tractor go back and forth in front of the house," she said, furious with herself for worrying.

Stephie tipped up her head and squinted at her mother. "Well, what do you want to do?" she asked innocently.

Mary Claire held her breath until the tractor cleared the narrow gate. "We'll make a picnic lunch!" she said on sudden inspiration. She caught Stephie's hand and headed for the house. "And when the boys get back, we'll go to that place Harley told you about and have a picnic."

"Yippee!" Stephie cried, skipping along at her mother's side.

Harley stopped the tractor on the drive at the side of the house to drop off Jimmy and was surprised to see Mary Claire and Stephie walking toward them, juggling a basket.

They waited patiently while he shut off the mower and tractor, then stepped closer as he swung to the ground.

"Well, you two girls look like cats who swallowed

canaries,'' he said as he pulled off his hat and wiped his forearm across the damp crease it had left on his forehead. ''What have you been up to?''

''We've been cooking,'' Stephie said proudly. ''We fried chicken and made deviled eggs and potato salad and we're gonna have a picnic in that spot by the creek you showed me.''

Harley lifted his brow. ''You are? Well, that sounds like a mighty good idea.'' He turned and offered Jimmy a helping hand as the boy jumped to the ground, then settled his hat back on his head. He put a finger on its brim and tipped it toward Mary Claire. ''I guess I'll be going, then. Y'all have a good time.''

''Harley, wait!''

He stopped at the sound of Mary Claire's voice and turned.

She sucked in a deep breath, her cheeks flaming, feeling awkward about offering an invitation to this man. ''We'd like for you to go with us...if you can spare the time,'' she said hesitantly.

A grin chipped at the corner of Harley's mouth. He was pleased she was including him in their plans. ''I'll make the time. Tell you what,'' he added. ''I'll drop the tractor by my house, pick up the pony and my horse and meet y'all over by the creek. That way, I can make good on my promise to give Stephie that ride.''

Though Mary Claire wasn't at all sure about Stephie's riding the pony, she nodded her agreement. ''We'll be there.''

With Stephie leading the way, Mary Claire and Jimmy followed her across the pasture and over the rise to a section of land Harley hadn't been able to mow. Huge rocks lay in huddled clumps, looking like crumbled castles in the bright sunlight. Choosing a spot close to the creek shaded by a live oak, Mary Claire spread out the blanket she'd brought. While the kids skipped stones across the creek's shallow water, Mary Claire dropped onto the blanket and began to lay out the food.

Stephie quickly grew bored with skipping stones and began to climb on the rocks. Making a game of it, she jumped from one huge boulder to the next, her hands flapping at shoulder height to keep her balance.

Harley saw her as he topped the rise and grinned at her childish antics. He stopped and watched, then returned her excited wave when she caught sight of him. Thinking he'd give her a ride back to the picnic spot where he saw Mary Claire kneeling on a blanket, he headed his horse toward Stephie. He laughed as he watched her hop from rock to rock, then almost lost his seat in the saddle when his horse suddenly shied.

"Whoa, boy," he soothed, tightening his grip on the reins. And then he heard it. The deathly rattle. Searching the rocks, he saw the snake poised on a flat surface not ten feet from where Stephie stood waiting for him. He quickly dropped the reins of the pony he led and kicked his horse into a run.

Mary Claire felt the ground tremble beneath her knees and looked up to see Harley racing his horse across the pasture. "What on earth is he up to?" she wondered out loud as she lifted a hand to shade her eyes. Then she saw Stephie standing on the jut of a low rock, and she lurched to her feet, sure he was about to run her down. "He's going to kill her!" she cried. Had he gone mad? Knowing she had to warn her daughter before she was crushed beneath the horse's hooves, she lunged forward, screaming, "Stephie! Run!"

Mary Claire stumbled and fell. Scrambling back to her feet, she screamed again, "Ste-phie!" But she was too late. Harley's horse bore down on her daughter, blocking her from view. Unable to watch her daughter trampled beneath the horse's hooves, Mary Claire clapped her hands over her eyes and dropped to her knees, sobbing.

A shot rang out, its sharp cry echoing through the trees. Mary Claire jerked her head up at the sound and saw Harley holding a rifle in his hand...and Stephie on the saddle in front of him.

On a sob, she clawed her way to her feet. "Stephie!" she cried brokenly. "Ste-phie!" She raced for the stand of rocks, and when she reached the horse's side, she snatched Stephie from Harley's arms, crushing her protectively against her chest as she backed away from him. "Are you crazy?" she screamed at Harley. "You could've killed her!"

Stephie's arms came around her mother's neck and her tears wet Mary Claire's cheeks. Mary Claire cradled the back of her head in her hand. "It's okay, baby," she soothed. "I've got you, now."

"Oh, Mama!" Stephie wailed. "It was a snake. And it was going to get me."

Mary Claire looked up, her gaze colliding with Harley's. "A snake?" she repeated.

Stephie's head bobbed against hers before she pulled back against her mother's arms. "Harley swung me up in the saddle and shot the snake, just like in the movies." She turned an adoring, if tear-filled, gaze to Harley. "Didn't you, Harley?"

For the life of him, Harley couldn't squeeze a word past the lump of fear that still lodged tight in his throat. He shoved the rifle he always carried back into the scabbard that hung from his saddle, then swung his leg over the horse's back and slid to the ground. He had to grab ahold of the saddle horn to keep his knees from buckling under him. With his forehead pressed hard against the side of the saddle, he couldn't remember a time in his life he'd ever been more scared.

A hand touched his shoulder. He turned to find Mary Claire standing behind him.

"I'm sorry," she murmured. "I thought..." She didn't finish, ashamed to tell Harley she'd thought he'd meant Stephie harm. But she saw the hurt in his eyes and knew that, without her voicing the words, somehow he knew. "Thank you," she said, then stood on tiptoe to press a kiss to his cheek. "You saved Stephie's life."

Embarrassed by her gratitude, Harley held out his arms to Stephie, who quickly leaned into them, link-ing her hands behind his neck and placing her own kiss on Harley's cheek. "You're my hero, Harley," she said solemnly, cupping his face with her small hands. "As long as forever, I'll remember you saved my life."

As far as rewards went, Harley couldn't have re-ceived one that touched him more.

And as far as excitement went, Harley felt he'd had more than his fair share. Seemed ever since Mary

Claire had moved to town, something was always happening. And for some reason, he was always caught smack-dab in the middle of the action.

Sometimes the action wasn't half-bad, like the picnic they'd gone on the day before. Though the run-in with the snake had put a damper on some of the fun, the outing had gone a long way in forging a new easiness between himself and Mary Claire. He'd enjoyed watching her with Stephie and Jimmy, seeing the love and protectiveness in her every move as she romped and played with them in the meadow. He'd enjoyed even more when she'd turned her laughing smile his way. But every time he thought about that snake all curled up ready to strike and Stephie standing there on that rock unaware, a shiver chased down his spine.

Sighing, he headed down the sidewalk to the barbershop, in desperate need of a haircut. "Hello, Will," he called out as he grabbed a magazine from the wall rack and dropped into a chair to wait his turn.

Will turned, clippers in hand, and gave him a brisk nod. "Afternoon, Harley. Be with you in a minute."

Harley crossed a boot over his knee and balanced the magazine across his propped leg. Lazily thumbing through the pages, something caught his eye, and he flipped back a page to see a picture of Carter's Mercantile spread across half a page. Cody Fipes stood on the street in front of the store, his hands on his hips, frowning at the camera, the star pinned on his chest catching the sun. Beneath the picture ran the headline TEMPTATION, TEXAS, ADVERTISES FOR WOMEN, and below it the subhead "Sheriff

strives to save dying town." Chuckling, Harley folded the magazine in half and began to read.

He hadn't read more than a paragraph when a shadow fell over the page, and he glanced up to see Cody standing in front of him, his hands on his hips, frowning, just like in the picture.

Harley chuckled and thumped the page with the back of his hand. "If you want to encourage women to move to Temptation you ought to try using a picture of Hank to entice 'em, instead of your ugly mug."

Cody dropped into the chair next to Harley with a frustrated sigh. "I tried. He wouldn't pose."

Harley chuckled again. "Can't say as I blame him."

"You here for a haircut?" Cody asked.

"Nah. Thought I'd get a tooth pulled."

Cody shot him a dark look. "Funny, Harley. Real funny."

Harley looked at him askance. "What's got you so down in the mouth?"

Cody gestured to the magazine Harley still held. "That, for starters. Every time I step out of my office, some reporter's shoving a microphone in front of my mouth or a camera's flashing in my face."

Harley shook his head, trying not to smile. "Being a hero can be a hell of an inconvenience for a man."

"I'm not any damn hero," Cody replied irritably. "I'm just a man trying to find a way to save his town." He frowned, crossing his arms over his chest and staring out the front window to the street outside. "And it's working, damn it. As much grief as I've taken over my idea, it's working."

Harley lifted a brow. "How so?"

"Two new families have already moved to town. A guy from up north, a plumber, moved in last week with his wife and kids, and a second family is moving here next week. The man's wife wants to open a clothing store here in Temptation."

Harley bit back a grin, ready to give Cody a hard time. "I thought your plan was to get *single* women to move to Temptation."

Cody narrowed his eyes at him. If looks could kill, Harley knew he'd be falling out of the chair stone-cold dead.

"There is Mary Claire Reynolds, you know," Cody replied, ready to give as good as he got. "She's single."

Already regretting his ribbing, Harley frowned. "Yeah, she is that."

"And she's starting a business, which is just what I'd hoped people would do."

Harley glanced up in surprise. "She is?"

Pleased that he knew something Harley didn't about his new neighbor, Cody settled back in his chair, buffed his fingernails on the thigh of his jeans and preened. "Yep. Saw her flier in the window over at Carter's Mercantile. She's setting up a bookkeeping service." He shifted his gaze to the barber. "Hey, Will! How long you gonna be?"

"Keep your shirt on, Cody. You don't want me cutting off Lou's ear now, do you?"

Lou lurched up from the chair, and Will grabbed the bib around his neck and hauled him back down.

Cody pushed himself to his feet. "I think I'll run

over and check the mail and then come back when there's not such a crowd.''

"I don't know why you're telling me,'' Will muttered disagreeably. "I ain't your secretary.''

Cody gave Harley's boot a shove, knocking his foot from his knee. "You hate paperwork, don't you, Harley? Maybe you ought to give Mary Claire a call and see if she'll keep your books for you.'' Seeing Harley's scowl, he sauntered out the door, grinning, pleased to know he'd gotten in the last jab.

Harley kept telling himself it wasn't Cody's prodding that had made him box up all his records a week later and head for Mary Claire's place with them. Hell, he didn't need an excuse to go see her—not that he wanted to see her of course. All he had to do was drop by to check on the land he'd leased, and he was almost sure to run into her or one of the kids.

He just needed a bookkeeper was all, he told himself. He was a rancher, not a damn accountant. He didn't have time for screwing around with balance sheets and income and expense reports and taxes. And, besides, he told himself, he suspected she could use the work. He didn't figure there were many folks in Temptation who required the services of a bookkeeper. And he'd rather pay her a helluva of a lot more than he would that accountant of his in San Antonio.

Knowing this, he tucked the box under his arm and strolled up the walk to Mary Claire's house, sure he was doing her a huge favor in offering her his business.

He knocked on the door, then waited, whistling

softly to himself the tune of the George Strait song that had been playing on the truck radio on the drive over.

Mary Claire opened the screen, a smile spreading across her face. "Well, if it isn't our hero." She pushed the door wider, inviting him in. "What are you doing here in the middle of the day? Don't you have cows to punch or damsels in distress to save?"

Harley grinned at her teasing, liking this change in Mary Claire. Ever since he'd rescued Stephie from the snake, she'd been nicer to him, more open. "I'm here on official business," he said with a nod at the box. "Saw your sign in the window at Carter's Mercantile and thought I'd throw a little business your way."

It was all Mary Claire could do to keep from clapping her hands in delight. "Well, in that case, come right in." She motioned for him to follow her into the study she'd created for herself in what was once her aunt Harriet's parlor. Sunshine flooded through the lace curtains, turning the walls she'd painted cream to the color of butter. She stepped behind the desk while Harley scooted the box across its polished top.

She dipped her head over the opened flaps. "What is all this?"

"My records."

Mary Claire lifted a fistful of invoices stained with coffee and God only knew what else. "These are records?" she asked, her nose wrinkling in disgust.

"Yes, ma'am," he said proudly. "Every invoice, bill and bank statement I've received this year."

Mary Claire dropped them and dug deeper, drawing

out a bank statement. Postmarked March 23, the envelope had never been opened. She eyed him warily. "When was the last time you reconciled your checkbook?"

Avoiding her gaze, he lifted a shoulder. "I don't know. A month or so ago, I guess."

She wagged the envelope beneath his nose. "It's almost July, and this envelope is dated March and has never been opened, so I'd venture to say it's been more than a month or so."

Harley frowned, not liking having his nose rubbed in the fact that he had a problem keeping his records up-to-date. Hell, he'd come to offer her work, not get a lecture on his shortcomings. "Maybe. I'm not sure," he replied reluctantly.

Mary Claire leaned across the desk, putting her face within inches of his. "Fess up, Harley. How far behind are you?"

Unable to look her in the eye, he stared at the floor instead, scuffing his toe against the braided rug. "Well, to be honest, I'm not much for keeping records. What I get, I throw in this box, and when the new year rolls around, I haul it all to my accountant and he figures out my income taxes for the year."

Mary Claire eyed the box and pursed her lips, thinking of the hourly fee the firm she'd worked for in Houston would've charged for such a job. "And I would imagine he charges you a small fortune for his time."

Harley dragged off his hat and blew out a long breath, remembering the bill he'd received from his accountant for the last year. "I guess that's a pretty fair assumption."

Mary Claire was tempted to pass the box right back to him, thinking of the nightmare involved in sorting out almost six months' worth of records. But she needed the work and knew if she did a good job, she could use Harley as a reference.

"It's going to cost you," she warned.

"Nothing's come free to me yet," he replied.

She hesitated a moment longer, then relented. "Oh, all right, you've got yourself a bookkeeper. But I expect you to bring me everything you receive in the way of bills, invoices or bank statements at least once a week. I'll charge you by the hour and send you a bill at the end of each month." She eyed the box and shook her head, thinking of the hours required to complete six months' worth of work in one. "But be prepared," she warned him. "That first bill is going to be a killer."

"I consider myself warned." Harley grinned and extended his hand. "A pleasure to do business with you, ma'am."

In spite of herself, Mary Claire laughed as she shook his hand. "You might not think so when you get my bill."

Five

Two days later, Harley found himself turning down Mary Claire's drive again, but this time instead of a box of receipts and canceled checks, he hauled a long gooseneck trailer filled with bawling cows. He'd separated the cows from their calves the day before, and the mama cows were none too happy with the arrangement. They'd bawled all night, keeping Harley awake while they'd walked the fence line, searching for their babies. Harley could've been angry about being robbed of his sleep, but he knew how they felt. He'd done his own share of bawling when Susan had taken his babies away from him.

He braked in front of the gate, half expecting Mary Claire and her kids to shoot out of the house to see what he was up to. But when they hadn't appeared by the time he'd swung open the gate, he began to

wonder if they'd heard him drive up. He looked toward the house, squinting against the bright sunshine,
but didn't see any movement.

She probably has them busy with chores, he told
himself, and strode back to his truck. But they'd be
along anytime now, likely before he made it through
the gate. If they hadn't heard his truck, the cows had
certainly done a good job at announcing his arrival.

He drove through the opening, made a large circle
until he'd aimed the hood of his truck back at the
gate and the cattle trailer toward the open pasture,
then braked again and shut off the engine. Stepping
from the truck, he crossed back to the gate, swung it
closed and started to lift the chain to lock it back into
place…then changed his mind.

He pushed it open wide enough to pass through,
latched it behind him and then headed for the house.
He knew the kids would want to see the cows un-
loaded and would be disappointed if he did the deed
without them there to watch.

He lifted his hand to the screen door and rapped
twice, then twisted around, sticking his hands in his
jeans pockets and ducking to get a clear shot of his
trailer and cows. He heard the shuffle of feet from the
other side of the door and turned back around, peering
through the fine mesh screen to see Mary Claire
standing opposite him. Her eyes were red and her
cheeks wet, and before Harley even thought about
what he was doing, he'd jerked open the screen door
and had his hands on her trembling shoulders.

"What's wrong?" he asked in a panic as he backed
her up a step. "What's happened?"

She lowered her head and squeezed her eyes shut,

by the elbow and aimed her for the door. "Come on," he said, herding her ahead of him. "We've got some cows to unload."

Mary Claire didn't remember ever feeling so dirty. Dust streaked her face and covered every inch of her clothing. She could even feel the fine granules on her teeth as she swept her parched tongue across her lips in a futile attempt to wet them.

Sighing, she dropped down onto the edge of the trailer bed. "Are we done?" she asked wearily.

Harley tipped back his hat and, pulling a red bandanna from his pocket mopped the sweat from his forehead. "Just about."

Mary Claire narrowed an eye at him, not relishing the thought of eating any more dust. "What do you mean 'just about'?"

"Well, I've got one cow penned up in my barn with mastitis. She needs her teats doctored."

Mary Clair shivered in revulsion. The very thought of putting her hands on a cow's teats made her stomach roll. She stood and dusted off her jeans. "If it's all the same to you, I think I'll pass."

Harley stuffed his bandanna back into his pocket. "Oh, I'll do the doctoring. I just need you to feed her baby."

Already headed for the gate and the house beyond, Mary Claire stopped and looked back. "Her baby?" she repeated, her interest piqued.

Harley grabbed the gate of the trailer and pulled it closed with a grinding of metal. "Yep. The calf can't nurse her mama because of the mastitis. If I don't feed the little fellow, he'll die of starvation."

Mary Claire worried her lip, her heart already going out to the poor calf. "And exactly how does one go about feeding a baby calf?" she asked, not wanting to obligate herself to the task until she knew exactly what was involved.

Harley chuckled as he strode over to her and clapped a companionable hand on her shoulder. "Don't worry. We won't be needing your plumbing as a substitute." He ducked, laughing, when Mary Claire took a swing at his head.

"Very funny, Harley," she muttered, but headed for his truck.

"Wasn't trying to be funny," he said innocently enough. "Just trying to ease your fears."

At the driver's side door, Mary Claire stopped and folded her arms across her breasts. "All right, so what *do* you use to feed the calf?"

"A bucket with a big long nipple on the side." He gave her a nudge, guiding her into the cab before she had time to refuse. "All you've got to do is hold the bucket."

And holding the bucket, Mary Claire soon learned, was no easy feat. The calf butted the bucket with his head, sending its sticky contents splashing across Mary Claire's hands and arms and dripping down her legs.

"Yuck! What is this stuff?" she cried, trying to get a better grip on the bucket.

"Calf starter. Kinda like baby formula," Harley explained from the opposite stall where he knelt, gently squeezing milk from the mama cow's engorged teats. "Stick your hand in it and rub some on the nipple so the calf can smell it. He'll take to the nipple a lot faster.''

Grimacing, Mary Claire dipped her fingers into the murky yellow liquid, then quickly wiped them down the length of the nipple. "Come on, baby,'' she urged, rubbing the nipple against the calf's nose. "Drink your dinner.''

The calf found the nipple and latched on, giving the bucket a good hard yank. Mary Claire tightened her fingers around the rim of the bucket, bracing her feet. A smile spread across her face. "I think he's got the hang of it," she whispered, not wanting to startle the calf.

His job finished, Harley stood at the stall wall behind her, watching. He smiled at her back, knowing he'd been right about keeping her busy. She hadn't mentioned the kids once in more than an hour. "I believe he has," he murmured.

Surprised to hear his voice so close, Mary Claire twisted around and saw him standing less than two feet away watching her closely through the slats of the stall. Heat flamed in her cheeks and she turned her attention back to the calf.

Within seconds, Harley was beside her, his hands joining hers along the bucket's rim, his shoulder brushing hers. "If you'll tip it just a little, he won't get so much air along with his milk.''

"Oh," she mumbled self-consciously, and did as he instructed. The calf continued to suck until he'd drained the bucket dry. Harley remained beside her, his shoulder and thigh pressed against hers, the warmth of his hands nearly burning a hole in hers where they touched. He smelled like sweat and sun-

shine and maybe just a little like the cows he'd un-
loaded, but Mary Claire found the scent surprisingly
seductive rather than repulsive.

Harley eased the nipple from the calf's mouth.
"He's done," he said unnecessarily. "I'll rinse out
the bucket."

He left, taking with him the heat of his hands and
her disturbing awareness of his body, and leaving her
feeling strangely alone. She squatted down eye level
with the calf. "Is your tummy full?" she asked and
reached out a tentative hand to rub his nose. He butted
her hand, catching her chin with his nose, knocking
her off balance. Mary Claire fell flat on her butt on
the scattered hay with a muffled "Oomph." A
chuckle behind her won a frown.

"Strong little cuss, isn't he?"

Mary Claire scrambled to her feet, dusting at the
hay that clung to her already filthy jeans. "You
might've warned me," she muttered.

Harley swung open the stall door, then waited for
her to pass through. "And interrupt your bonding?"
He chuckled again when she shot him a glare. He
threw an arm around her shoulders, letting the door
click closed behind them. He guided her out of the
barn, using the weight of his arm to keep her at his
side. He was surprised, but not close to being sorry
that she allowed him that bit of familiarity. When they
stepped outside, the sun was already sinking below
the treetops. "How about a beer?" he asked compan-
ionably.

Though Mary Claire had never particularly enjoyed
the taste of beer, at the moment a cold one sounded
like heaven. She was hot and thirsty and the thought

of going home to her empty house was about as appealing as unloading another load of dust-churning cattle. "Sounds wonderful," she said on a sigh.

He led her to the house, about three hundreds yards south of the barn. It was a large, ranch-style place, made of native limestone with a tin roof much like the one that topped her house, though she could tell this one was a lot newer. The setting sun cast its red-gold glow across the slanted roof, turning the tin coppery in color. At the back step, Harley stopped and scraped his boots down the length of a piece of metal, knocking off most of the dust and mud that caked his boots. Then he shucked them.

Mary Claire looked at her once-white tennis shoes and knew that scraping them wouldn't come close to cleaning them. She stooped and hooked a hand over one heel, then the other, peeling off the ruined shoes.

Harley held the door open and let her pass in front of him. She stepped into his kitchen, her curiosity making her momentarily forget about the offered beer. Though clean and sparsely decorated, the kitchen still somehow managed to look cluttered. Mail was scattered across the counter, and a solitary plate and cup rested on the dish drainer. The table that stood in the center of the room had a messy assortment of papers littering its surface. Shadowed squares on the wall told her that pictures had once hung there. She stopped and simply stared, feeling the loneliness in the room wrap itself around her heart.

"It's not much, but it's home," Harley said, and gave her a gentle nudge toward the sink. "We can wash up here." He hit the handle on the faucet with the back of his wrist, lathered up, then passed the bar of soap to her. Dipping her hands under the water, Mary Claire rubbed the bar between her palms, painfully aware of the man who stood at her side and the big, nearly empty house he called home. He rinsed, then stepped out of her way, grabbing a cloth from the counter to dry his hands. Mary Claire stole another glance at the solitary plate and cup in the drainer and felt her heart contract. Then she, too, turned away, dripping water on the floor.

Harley tossed her the towel and headed for the table. He pulled out a chair and knocked a sweat-stained hat off its seat. "Have a seat and I'll get us that beer."

He padded to the refrigerator in his stocking feet, pulled out two long-neck beers, popped the caps and crossed back to the table. Using his elbow as a rake, he cleared a spot on the table in front of Mary Claire, set down the beer, then whipped out the chair next to hers and straddled it. His knee bumped hers, and Mary Claire jumped at the unexpected contact.

"Sorry," he said, but didn't bother to move his knee. He tipped his beer toward her and gave her a wink. "Thanks for your help this afternoon. Made the unloading a lot faster and a helluva lot easier."

She closed her fingers around her beer to still the trembling the pressure of his knee against her thigh had created in them. "You're welcome...I think." Fighting the need to squirm, she glanced down at her dust-covered clothes and grimaced. "Is your work always this dirty?"

Harley chuckled. "No. Sometimes it's worse."

She groaned. "I'd hate to have to keep up with your laundry."

He chuckled again and took a sip of his beer, then let it dangle between two fingers over the top of the chair back. "Keeping it simple is the ticket," he explained. "Every night when I come in, I strip off my clothes in the laundry room there," he said, nodding toward a darkened doorway, "and put everything in the washer, underwear and all. While it's washing, I cook myself something to eat. By that time, the washer's finished and I toss it all into the dryer, eat my dinner, then head for the shower and bed. Next morning, I pluck my clothes out of the dryer, put 'em back on, then repeat the process that night."

Mary Claire's gaze remained fixed on the darkened doorway he'd indicated. She could almost see him stripping off his clothes, walking back out and strutting around the kitchen buck naked while preparing his solitary dinner. The image did something to her ability to swallow, for the beer she'd just sipped slid down her throat unaided, and she choked.

Harley reached over and thumped her on the back while she coughed. "Did your beer have a bone it?" he asked, looking at her with a teasing glint in his eye.

Dragging in a breath, she shook her head. "No, it just went down the wrong way." She tried another swallow.

"Better?" he asked, studying her intently.

"Yes," she said, then added dryly, "but I think you owe me an apology."

He lifted a brow. "I do?"

"Yes! For chastising me for walking around in my backyard in my nightgown when you prance around your kitchen in nothing but your birthday suit."

Harley just grinned. "But there's nobody around to see me naked."

Mary Claire frowned at him. "What if somebody dropped by unexpectedly?"

"Nobody drops by here, 'cept for maybe Cody, and I assure you," he added, his grin deepening, "I don't have anything he hasn't seen before."

Mary Claire's cheeks flamed and she glanced away. But her gaze landed on that damn dish drainer again, with its single plate and cup, a vivid reminder of the lonely life Harley led—and the times she'd resented his presence at her own house and table. Guilt stabbed at her for her selfishness. And to think that Harley had caught her crying like a baby because her children were going to be gone for one measly weekend when he spent every day of his life alone.

"I appreciate you taking me under your wing today," she murmured, dropping her gaze to her beer. "If you hadn't, I probably would've spent the entire day moping around the house, missing Stephie and Jimmy."

Harley nodded knowingly. "I figured as much. Keeping busy helps."

Mary Claire knew from the tone of his voice that he spoke from experience. "How often do you get to see your children?" she asked softly.

"Like your husband, I was given a weekend a month. Unlike him, I took advantage of every one." He shook his head sadly, remembering. "But that didn't last long. Once they settled in, the kids both got busy with friends and activities and they resented having to come here and missing out on so much." He shrugged. "So I started going to San Antonio and checking into a hotel for the weekend and taking whatever time they could give me.''

That he would go to such lengths to spend time with his children touched Mary Claire. She placed a hand over his. ''I'm sorry.''

The warmth of her hand seeped into Harley's, bringing with it a comfort that worked its way clear to his soul. But as he tipped his face to hers and looked into the depths of eyes as green as new spring leaves, he realized he wanted more from her than her sympathy. He wanted all of her.

Holding her gaze, measuring her reaction, he slowly turned his hand over beneath hers and laced his fingers with hers. Her eyes widened a bit, her fingers twitched…and then she curled them around his, accepting him, while her eyes turned a darker green.

''Mary Claire,'' he said, his voice suddenly husky, ''I know I promised I'd never do it again, but I sure would like to kiss you right now.''

She felt the warmth spread from her heart to the tips of her toes, and though her stomach tightened into a nervous knot at the thought of his kissing her again, she realized she wanted the same thing. ''I'd like that, too, Harley,'' she whispered.

Bracing his hands on the back of the chair, he lifted himself slightly from the seat and leaned forward. She closed her eyes, nearly blinded by the heat of his gaze, as his face drew nearer. His touch was light at first, his mustache tickling the tender flesh around her lips. His tongue darted out, tracing her mouth from corner to corner, teasing her lips to open for him. When they did, he deepened the kiss, slowly drawing her in. She tasted the loneliness in him, felt it in the hesitant sweep of his tongue. She lifted her hands to his face, wanting to assure him that he wasn't alone. Not tonight. She was here with him.

She felt the vibrating rumble of a groan against her lips, then he was pushing out of his chair, kicking it aside and hauling her up and into his arms. She clung to him, feeling the desperation in the wide hands that moved across her back pulling her tighter against him, feeling the need in the urgent thrust of his tongue, and answered with a desperation and need of her own.

Knowing he was quickly losing control, Harley lifted his hands and knotted them in the hair at her temples as he drew away to meet her gaze. "God help me, Mary Claire," he murmured. "But I want to make love with you."

She circled his wrists with her hands, and a soft tremulous smile curved her lips as she looked up into his eyes. "God help us both, then, because I want the same thing."

The flicker of surprise in his eyes was there and gone so fast Mary Claire wasn't sure she'd even seen it. Then, without warning, he reached down, caught her beneath her knees and lifted her up into his arms. Mary Claire squealed in surprise, wrapping her arms around his neck to keep from falling as he strode from the kitchen and down a dark hall.

"But, Harley," she reminded him breathlessly, "we're filthy."

He grinned, but kept walking. "I know." He pushed open a door with his stocking foot, slamming it against the wall, but didn't even slow down. Mary Claire thought she saw the shadow of a long wide bed in the darkness before another door slapped against a wall at his foot's urging. He lifted his elbow and hit a switch and light flooded the room. Mary Claire looked around the tiled bathroom, then cupped his cheek with one hand and turned his face to hers.

"Are you thinking what I think you're thinking?" she asked nervously.

He planted a kiss on her lips and said, "Depends on what you're thinking." He lowered her to her feet and swung open the shower door. Leaning inside, he twisted on the faucet with one hand while he used the other to undo the buttons of his shirt. He stepped back out, tugged his shirttail free of his jeans, exposing a wide expanse of bare chest. "Takes a minute or two for the water to heat," he explained, then pulled her into his arms again.

Her heart thundering, Mary Claire laid a hand against the soft pelt of hair on his chest, trying to still her sudden attack of nerves. Making love in a darkened bedroom was one thing, but showering together in a bathroom flooded with light seemed so much more...intimate. A shiver chased down her spine.

Harley felt it beneath his hand. "Are you cold?" he asked, pushing her to arm's length to peer at her.

"No, just a little nervous," she replied honestly.

An understanding smile curved beneath his mustache. "I promise not to splash soap in your eyes."

His gentle teasing went a long way in reassuring her, but those bright lights continued to trouble her. "Do you have any candles?" she asked hesitantly.

"Candles?" Harley repeated, then cursed his lack of sensitivity, realizing a woman like Mary Claire would want a more romantic setting than a bathroom with bold fluorescent lighting and the scent of Irish

Spring soap. He gave her elbows a squeeze, then released her. "Stay right here. I'll be back in a minute."

Alone in the bathroom, Mary Claire hugged her arms beneath her breasts and stared at the steam billowing above the shower door. She wondered if she hadn't been a little hasty in agreeing to this. She was attracted to Harley, she couldn't argue that, but what did she really know about him?

The lights suddenly snapped off, throwing the room into darkness. Mary Claire was so startled she stumbled forward, reaching out a hand for the shower door to steady herself. The scrape of a match made her turn, and she saw Harley in the match's tiny glow touching the flame to a lantern's wick.

Grinning shyly behind the lantern's soft light, he lifted one shoulder in a shrug. "I don't have any candles, but thought this might serve the same purpose."

At that moment Mary Claire realized how much she really did know about this man. He was kind and gentle and thoughtful, and so handsome he made her heart ache. She opened her arms to him.

Harley set the lantern on the floor and stepped into the circle she'd created for him, drawing her close. The feel of his arms around her chased away the last of her doubts. Boldly, she stepped from his embrace and began to work the buttons free on her blouse.

Harley watched, his blue eyes turning smoky as she slipped the blouse from her slender shoulders and let it fall to the floor. He lifted a hand to cup a lace-covered breast and murmured, "So soft." He returned his gaze to her eyes. "And as beautiful as I'd imagined."

His hand slid from her breast to the snap on her

jeans. The snap popped open beneath his fingers, the sound of its release followed by the metallic grate of her zipper as he pushed it in a slow, aching journey downward. His knuckles grazed her bare skin, making her shiver. Stepping closer, he slipped his hands inside the denim and urged the stiff fabric down along with her silk panties. His lips followed their descent, pressing kisses to her thighs, her knees, her shins. He knelt at her feet, holding her jeans open while she stepped out of them.

He rose, holding her with his gaze, until he stood almost eye to eye with her again. Hungry for her taste, he covered her mouth with his as he fumbled for the clasp of her bra. Once freed, he tossed it aside and quickly shucked off his own shirt and jeans. Naked, his eyes never once leaving her face, he stood before her and held out his hand.

He seemed so calm, so relaxed, so comfortable with his nudity and his intent. Taking a deep breath, Mary Claire twined her fingers with his. Together they stepped under the shower's spray, turning once again into each other's arms.

Steam hissed around them, misting the shower doors, creating a private haven for the lovers. Harley, his mouth locked on Mary Claire's, groped for the bar of soap in the dish on the wall and lathered his hands behind her back. Starting at the nape of her neck, he worked his hands in slow burning circles across her shoulders and down her back. At her buttocks, his hands slowed, then cupped the rounded mounds, massaging her bare flesh as he drew her flush against him.

Slick and hot and oh, so clever, his fingers slipped

between her legs, finding the sensitive button that sent heat racing through her veins until she all but burned with her need for him. She moaned against his lips and arched against him, glorying in the thrust of his engorged manhood against the slope of her pelvis.

Needing to touch him as thoroughly as he'd touched her, she backed away, taking the soap from his hands. She lathered quickly and spread her hands across his chest, shaping the firm swell of his muscles, then moving down his strong arms and back up until her hands met again in the center of his chest. Feeling the fast kick of his heart beneath her palms, she lifted her gaze to his. What she saw there in the depths of those smoky blue eyes gave her courage.

Smiling provocatively, she took her hands on a slow journey downward, fanning them out across the flat plane of his stomach, pausing to dip her finger into his navel and then moving farther still until the heels of her hands bumped against his arousal.

The pulsing hardness against her palms was both terrifying and exhilarating. Drawing a shuddery breath, she curled her fingers around the heat and watched his eyes close and his head fall back. Up and down, around and around, she moved her soap-slickened hands in a mindless journey with no thought for anything but his pleasure.

Harley stood it as long as he could, then, on a groan, he caught her hand in his, stilling its erotic movements. "Careful. I can't hold on much longer."

Ignoring the warning, Mary Claire pressed her body against his. "I don't want you to," she whispered as water rivered between their bodies.

Growling low in his throat, he caught her buttocks

in his hands again and lifted, bringing her with him as he braced his shoulder blades against the wall. He lifted her higher, then closed his mouth over her breast, drawing her nipple deep into his mouth. The gentle suckling stole her breath. With a low, guttural moan, Mary Claire dug her fingers into his hair and clung as an echoing sensation stabbed at her feminine core.

Wanting, needing to feel him inside her, she wrapped her legs around his waist. Forcing his face from her breast, she pressed her mouth to his, telling him without words her need. He lowered her slowly, guiding her until his hardness butted against her feminine opening. Gently he eased inside.

"Oh, God, Mary Claire," he groaned as he felt her hot velvet flesh close around him. But those were the only words he managed to get out before she started moving against him, urging him to follow in the age-old dance. His breath shortened to grabbing gasps, and his arms tightened around her as he thrust his body against hers again and again and again. Water continued to pelt his face and arms, but he was oblivious to its needlelike sting, every fiber of his being focused on nothing but giving her pleasure.

He felt the first tremor within her, a shiver of sensation against his heated flesh. The explosion followed, silent but deafening in its intensity, debilitating in its powerful surge as he felt her pulsations suck at him, drawing him with her over the edge.

His knees gave way to the weakness, and he took her with him as he slid down the shower wall, gathering her into his arms as he sank to the tiled floor. With his head tipped against hers, he cradled her against him and held her until the shudders ceased.

Six

"Harley?"

"Mmm?"

"The water's getting cold."

He opened one eye, then let it drift closed again, as if even that small effort took more energy than he possessed. "So it is," he murmured, and found the strength to nuzzle her neck with his nose.

She caught him by the ears, laughing, and pulled his face to hers. "We're going to freeze if we don't get out of here soon."

He sighed, shifting her hip more fully against his groin. "You're probably right," he said with regret. Bracing a hand on the wall for support, he heaved himself to his feet, bringing Mary Claire up with him. He ducked his head under the cold spray and stretched to twist off the faucet, then did a full body shake, sending the icy droplets of water flying from his body while Mary Claire shivered beside him.

Jerking down towels draped over the door, he tossed one to Mary Claire, then briskly rubbed his wet skin, grinning at her while she did the same. "Clean?" he asked.

She laughed again, looking at the wrinkled skin on her arms. "More like a prune."

Chuckling, Harley caught her hand, pushed open the door and led her across the tiled floor, pausing only long enough to pick up the lantern.

At the side of the bed, he stopped and placed the lantern on the nightstand. After whipping back the covers, he turned and pulled her to him. She felt the low moan start somewhere deep inside him and work its way up his throat until it vibrated against her lips. "Now that we're clean," he murmured huskily against her mouth, "I can make love with you."

Startled, Mary Claire looked at the bathroom door, then back at him. "But you just did."

A grin chipped at one corner of his mouth as he cupped her buttocks with his hands and tugged her up against his arousal. "That, my dear, was merely foreplay."

Saturday afternoon, Mary Claire sat on the floor of her den in front of the television, Harley's box of papers snugged up against her knee. Small stacks of paper were laid in a semicircle in front of her as she methodically worked to empty the box's contents, sorting the papers into different piles.

Though they'd spent the night at Harley's house, Mary Claire had insisted on returning to her own home that morning, fearing her children would call and she wouldn't be there to answer the phone.

"Harley Kerr, you should be ashamed," she lectured him.

Stretched out on the couch behind her, his eyes at half-mast as he lazily watched the New York Yankees threaten the winning record of the Texas Rangers, Harley yawned. "For what?"

She twisted around to frown at him. "For being such a poor businessman."

Insulted, Harley pushed to an elbow. "I beg your pardon!"

Mary Claire waved a hand at the papers in front of her. "Well, what would you call this mess?"

Harley sank back down, tucking a hand under his cheek as he let his eyes drift closed. "A disorganized mess, but that sure as hell doesn't make me a poor businessman."

With a frustrated huff of breath, Mary Claire shook her head, reached back into the box and pulled out a thick ledger. Spreading it open across her knees, she flipped through the pages. The ledger was dated December 31 of the previous year, and it had obviously been prepared by someone other than Harley, for it was divided into neat distinct sections. Assets. Liabilities. Income and Expenses. Each section was computer generated and filled with long rows and columns of numbers.

Hoping to familiarize herself with Harley's previous accountant's methods, she quickly scanned each page. Under Assets were listed his home, his acreage, the outbuildings scattered around his property. Tractors and equipment followed, along with an inventory of the cattle he currently owned and the balances of several different bank accounts. The numbers beside each were impressive, the total, staggering. On paper at least, the man was worth well over a million! He was a simple man, and she would never have dreamed he was worth so much. Stealing a glance his way, she saw that his eyes were closed.

With a shake of her head, she flipped to the Liabilities section, expecting to find another long list, negating the Assets. Notes owed for equipment and cattle. A mortgage on his home and land. But none of those things were there. She found only two listings. One, a loan from the bank in Temptation for ten thousand dollars. She quickly dug through the stacks of papers scattered on the floor until she found the accompanying papers from the bank. Spreading them open against the ledger, she soon realized that nothing but Harley's signature had been required to guarantee the note.

Returning to the ledger, she discovered the second liability was under the name of Susan Kerr Hendrix. The amount beside the name stole Mary Claire's breath. Why did he owe his ex-wife such an exorbitant sum of money? she wondered.

She quickly turned to the Income and Expenses section. The items listed for Income were all generated from cattle and hay sales. The Expenses column was another story. Granted, there were the expected feed and grain bills, monies paid to a veterinarian and to an equipment company in a nearby town, along with a list of other sundry items. But it was the monthly amount paid to Susan Kerr Hendrix that held her attention.

Child support? she wondered, and stole another glance Harley's way. His hand pillowed beneath his cheek, he slept, his chest rising and falling in the relaxed rhythm of sleep. Telling herself she wasn't being nosy—after all, Harley had given her the records himself—she turned back to the ledger and bent her head over them. It couldn't be just child support, she thought, studying the amount and the regularity with which it was paid. Alimony? No, she decided, with a quick shake of her head. Since the name Hendrix followed the name Kerr, his ex-wife had obviously remarried and would no longer be eligible for alimony. So why was he paying her?

Giving herself a shake, she set the ledger aside and reached back into the box. It's none of my business, she told herself. My job is to keep his books. Period. Money he sends his ex-wife is no concern of mine.

But though she willed herself otherwise, the question "Why?" continued to buzz around in her head.

Gathering the ledger and as many stacks of papers as she could carry in her hands, she tiptoed from the den and made her way to her study. She switched on her computer, then returned to the den for another load while it booted up. With the papers scattered across her desktop in neat stacks, she began to set up his accounts, using the two years' experience she'd gathered at the firm she'd worked for in Houston and the software program she'd invested in as her guide.

She was so intent in her work she didn't hear Harley slip into the study hours later and move up behind her chair.

His cheek brushed hers, startling her. "A burglar

could strip this house bare and you'd never be the wiser.''

She leaned back in the chair, rolled her shoulders and sighed, lifting a hand to his opposite cheek. "I doubt that.''

Liking the feel of her soft hand against his skin, Harley turned his face, catching her hand in his and pressing a kiss against the palm. "Wanna mess around?''

She twisted her head to stare at him, her eyes widening in surprise. "Harley Kerr! You are insatiable!''

He grinned and a blush reddened his cheeks. "Nah. Just can't seem to get enough of you.''

She spun the chair around and caught his belt buckle, pulling him into her lap.

Trying not to put his full weight on her, he teased her with a smile. "Haven't you got this backward? Isn't it the boss who's supposed to have his secretary on his lap?''

Mary Claire locked her arms around his neck and pulled his face down to hers. "I'm not your secretary. I'm your bookkeeper.''

His mustache tickled her mouth as he brushed his lips over hers. "Same difference.''

The heat was instantaneous, flaming to life low in her abdomen, making Mary Claire sigh against his mouth. "You do realize you're interrupting my work, don't you?'' she asked, though the complaint was halfhearted at best.

His tongue snaked out and traced the curve of her lips. "Keep the clock running. I'll pay.''

Mary Claire laughed and gave his chin a playful

shove. "Don't you need to check your cows or something?"

He sighed. "Reckon I should." He gave her a hopeful smile. "You'll come with me, won't you?"

Mary Claire glanced at the computer screen where her cursor blinked lazily and knew she'd rather be with Harley than alone in her office crunching numbers. "Do I get to feed the calf?"

"I suppose I could allow you that privilege."

Within minutes she'd shut off her computer and was walking alongside Harley to his truck. He opened the driver's door and held it while she climbed inside, but he remained outside. "We'll cut across the pasture and check the cows before we head over to my place. I'll open the gate and you drive through."

Unfamiliar with the truck's controls, Mary Claire pressed in the clutch, turned the key in the ignition, then shifted into first. Pleased with her accomplishment, she smiled at Harley as she drove past him through the open gate.

When he opened the truck door, she started to slide across the seat to the passenger side, but he caught her arm, pulling her back to his side.

Delighted that he wanted her close, Mary Claire rested a hand on his knee. They rode in companionable silence, bouncing their way across the uneven pasture while Harley did a silent count of his cows. When he was satisfied they were all there, he headed for his own acreage and the barn beyond.

As they drove, Mary Claire thought about that odd payment he made each month to his wife. Knowing she wouldn't be satisfied until she'd discovered the reason for it, she decided the simplest thing to do was just ask. Which she did as soon as they got to the barn.

"Harley?" she said as she climbed down from the truck after him. "When I was working on your books, I noticed a payment you make each month to your ex-wife. How do you want me to classify that?"

Harley's shoulders tensed and he turned away, busying himself by pulling a roll of barbed wire from the back of the truck. "It's a liability," he muttered.

"I know that," Mary Claire said in frustration. "But what's it for?"

When he turned to her, his eyes were as hard as glass. "Does it matter?"

"N-no," she stammered, then stamped her foot at her own cowardliness. "Well, of course it does. If I'm going to keep your books, I need to know how and why you spend your money."

Harley stared at her a moment, a muscle ticking on his jaw. "It's part of our divorce settlement," he said tightly, then wheeled and headed for the barn.

Mary Claire stared at his retreating back, then bolted to catch up with him. "Your divorce settlement? But I thought you'd been divorced for years?"

"Ten to be exact," he replied tersely. He tossed the roll of barbed wire into a corner, then grabbed the bucket and started mixing the starter milk for the calf. "When we divorced, Susan wanted half of everything I owned. Didn't matter that the farm had been in my family for years. The courts decided that she was entitled to half its value. I didn't have the cash and refused to sell out in order to pay her off, so at the court's insistence, I agreed to pay her monthly until the debt was fulfilled." In disgust, he tossed down the stick he'd used to stir the milk and caught up the bucket. "Like I said," he concluded, turning to frown at Mary Claire, "it's a liability." He shoved the bucket into her hands and stalked away.

Feeling as if his anger was directed at her in some way, Mary Claire entered the stall where the calf stood waiting for his dinner. From the stall next to her, she could hear the murmur of Harley's voice as he soothed the calf's mother.

"Here, baby," she whispered, offering the bucket. "Drink your milk."

The calf latched on to the nipple immediately and began to suck. Mary Claire stole a glance at Harley through the narrow slats. He was squatting beside the cow and had her swollen teats in his hands. She could see the tension in his shoulders, tension she had put there with her prying questions. But his touch remained gentle and his low voice soothing as he murmured words of comfort to the sick cow.

Mary Claire felt the spurt of tears to her eyes. That he was kind and gentle she'd already known. That he was fair and honest was evident in the regularity of the payments he made to his ex-wife. And now she had gone and upset him with her prying.

"Harley?" she called out softly.

"What?" came his terse reply.

"I'm sorry."

She watched his shoulders rise and fall in frustration. "You don't have anything to be sorry for," he mumbled.

The calf gave an impatient yank and Mary Claire looked down to find the bucket empty. Setting it aside, she slipped from the stall and stepped into the one where Harley worked. "Yes, I do," she said, and laid a hand on his shoulder. His muscles tensed beneath her touch. Forcing herself to keep her hand in place, she continued, "I brought up a subject that's obviously painful for you and I'm sorry about that."

Slowly the muscles beneath her hand relaxed. Rocking back on his heels, he twisted partway around and looked up at her. "What happened between Susan and me has nothing to do with you. What galls my soul is that I have to pay her with profits earned from a place she hated and couldn't wait to get away from." He shook his head sadly and turned back to the cow. "She never lifted a hand to help me work the place. Spent her days in the house, biding her time and secretly planning her escape while I worked my butt off making the place pay."

With no words of comfort left to offer, Mary Claire dropped to her knees beside him and rested her head against his shoulder while he continued to squeeze milk from the cow's swollen teats.

"Mama! We're home!"

Mary Claire jumped up from the table as the front door slammed, nearly knocking Harley down in her rush to see her children. She pushed past him, barreling down the hall and scooping Stephie up into her arms.

"Oh, I missed you, Stephie!" she cried, squeezing her daughter to her.

Harley stood behind them watching, smiling, patiently waiting his turn for a hug. The front door slammed again and Harley glanced up to see Jimmy charging for his mother. A man followed close on his heels—and Harley wished he'd remained in the kitchen and avoided this meeting. The man looked slicker than a used-car salesman and was dressed like a damn gigolo. His hair was all greased back like some kind of Italian movie star, and the silk shirt he wore was unbuttoned halfway down his chest, revealing a thick gold chain and a triangle of hairless chest. It was all Harley could do to keep from spitting on the floor at the man's feet.

Stephie stretched out her arms for Harley. "Harley! I had the bestest time in Houston!"

His gaze locked on the scowling face of the man opposite him, who was doing his own job of sizing Harley up, Harley held out his arms. Stephie leapt into them while Mary Claire gave Jimmy a hug. The man's scowl deepened as Stephie's arms circled Harley's neck.

"You did?" he asked, tearing his gaze away from the man to smile down at Stephie. "What did you do?"

"We went ice-skating at the Galleria, spent the day at Astro World, ate Mexican food at the coolest place and went to the movies," she finished breathlessly.

"Did you sleep any?" he teased.

Stephie giggled, giving Harley's shoulder a shove. "Of course I did, silly."

"Who's your friend, Mary Claire?" the man asked curtly.

Mary Claire glanced over the top of Jimmy's head to look at her ex-husband, her eyes wide with surprise. She'd never heard that jealous tone of voice from Pete before, but then again, she'd never given him reason to be jealous. "This is Harley Kerr, our neighbor. Harley,'' she said, glancing Harley's way, ''this is the children's father, Pete Reynolds.''

Though he would rather have ignored his upbringing, Harley shifted Stephie to his hip and extended his hand in greeting. ''Pleased to meet you,'' he murmured politely, though he knew it was a lie.

The man put a little more muscle than was necessary into the shake, and Harley gave back as good as he got, secretly pleased when he saw the guy wince.

Pete stepped back, flexing his fingers. ''The kids' bags are in the trunk,'' he mumbled sourly.

Mary Claire stood. ''I'll help you get them.''

''I will,'' Harley offered, carefully setting Stephie on her feet.

''No,'' Mary Claire said, stopping him with a hand on his arm. ''I think I'd better.''

Harley watched her follow Pete out the door and fought the stab of jealousy. ''There're cookies fresh from the oven on the table,'' he told the kids, then crossed to the front door while they raced for the kitchen.

Standing with one leg cocked and his hand braced against the doorjamb, he watched as Pete Reynolds lifted the trunk of a shiny Lexus and jerked out a bag. He could see the man's mouth moving as he tossed the bag to the ground, but couldn't quite make out his words. That he was mad about something was obvious in his jerky movements as he dove for another bag and threw it on top of the first. Slamming down the trunk, he wheeled to face Mary Claire, his face twisted in anger. Legs akimbo, her hands folded beneath her breasts, she faced him defiantly.

When Harley heard the word ''whore,'' he jerked

his hand from the doorjamb and slapped the screen open. He didn't need to hear any more. That the man had dared to insult Mary Claire was enough. His eyes narrowed on the two, he strode down the sidewalk, his steps hard and fast on the chipped bricks.

Pete lifted a hand, balling it into a fist, and Harley broke into a run, vaulting the fence and catching the man's hand before it hit its mark—Mary Claire's face. "I wouldn't do that if I were you," he said.

Pete tried to twist free. "This is none of your damn business."

"I just made it my business," Harley replied, his voice quiet but deadly. "Why don't you just climb back into that fancy car of yours and leave before I have to mess up your pretty face?"

Pete twisted free, massaging the hand Harley had grabbed, his eyes shooting fire. That he wanted to fight was obvious, but something he saw in Harley's eyes must have changed his mind, because he turned on his heel and marched to the opposite side of the car, yanked open the door and climbed in. With a roar of the engine, he jerked the car into reverse and spewed rocks as he shot back down the drive.

From behind him Harley heard Mary Claire's sigh of relief.

He turned to her. "Are you okay?"

She lifted her gaze to his. "I'm fine." She sighed again, shifting her gaze to follow the car's departure. "He's never done that before," she murmured, almost to herself. "He's been angry, but he's never lifted a hand to hit me before."

Harley watched, too, as the car grew smaller and

smaller in the distance, despising the man inside. "He called you a whore."

"He's called me worse."

"Not within my hearing," Harley said fiercely, turning to her. He cupped her cheek, the gentleness in his touch a strong contrast to the anger in his voice. "He was mad because I was here, wasn't he?"

Mary Claire nodded. Reaction was setting in. Tears filled her eyes and her chin trembled visibly. "Odd, isn't it?" she said, her voice quivering. "Never once in the years we were married did I cheat on him, and he cheated every chance he got. Yet, he called *me* a whore."

His heart breaking, Harley hauled her against his chest. "You're not a whore, Mary Claire. Don't ever let him make you believe that. You're a lady, through and through."

Whore. Whore. Whore.

Harley couldn't get the sound of Pete's voice out of his head. The word rolled around and around in his mind, eating at him, because he knew it was his presence that had spawned it.

Unable to sleep, he got up, saddled his horse and headed across the field for Mary Claire's house, using the moon's soft glow to light his way. He knew she was probably sleeping, but he just wanted to be near her. Not to see her, not to talk her, just be near her, if only to look at the window of the room where he knew she slept.

A cow bawled as he passed. An owl hooted from a far tree. Harley ignored them and urged his horse into a trot.

As he'd expected, the house was dark when he approached. He swung down off his horse and tied him to the gate. Climbing the fence, he hopped down and strode to the front of the house where he could look up at Mary Claire's window.

The window was open, the lace curtains slapping gently against the screen in the night breeze. Beside the window, he knew, was her bed. Folding his arms across his chest, he closed his eyes, imagining her sleeping as she had slept curled against him the past two nights, her hand tucked beneath the pillow, her bare bottom pressed against his groin. He sighed and opened his eyes.

And there she was, a shadow behind the screen, standing with her hand gripping a lace panel of the curtain. "Harley?" she whispered.

"Yeah, it's me," he said, embarrassed.

"What are you doing down there?"

"I couldn't sleep."

"Me, neither," came her soft reply. "Stay there. I'll be right down." Then she was gone.

His heart thundering against his ribs, Harley crossed to the front porch and climbed the steps. He stopped when the door opened and closed softly. Like a ghost, she seemed to float on a beam of moonlight across the porch toward him. Her hands reached up, framing his face, and the moon kissed her cheeks. "Hold me," she whispered. "Please, hold me."

Harley wrapped his arms around her and tucked her head under his chin, rocking her slightly. On a sigh, she laid a hand over his heart. "I missed you," she whispered.

"I missed you, too," he whispered back.

She laughed softly, rubbing her cheek against his chest. "How long have you been gone? Three hours? Four?"

"A lifetime."

She backed up a step, her hand still resting against his chest. "Did it seem that long to you, too?" she asked, her eyes filled with wonder.

"At least that long. I couldn't sleep. I wanted you in my bed with me."

She sagged against his chest, placing her cheek where her hand had rested before. "Me, too."

"Mary Claire?"

She glanced up and saw the question in his eyes. "We can't," she said, her voice full of regret. "The kids. I wouldn't know how to explain your presence in my bed in the morning."

He dropped his head, knowing she was right.

She placed a finger beneath his chin and lifted. "But there are other ways." Taking his hand, she led him around to where the porch ran along the side of the house. It was here she'd installed the wicker swing she'd hauled down from the attic. She urged him to a sitting position on the swing, then hiked up her nightgown and straddled him. That she wasn't wearing anything underneath became painfully obvious as she scooted across his lap.

Harley could barely breathe. "Mary Claire? What are you doing?"

She pressed a finger against his lips, then replaced it with her lips. Shifting her weight to her knees, she lifted her hand to the first button at the scooped neck of her gown.

When he realized her intent, Harley groaned

against her mouth and joined his hands with hers until together they'd bared a breast. Taking its weight in his hand, he rubbed his thumb across the nipple until it budded into a tight knot. Mary Claire arched, letting her head drop back, and purred like a cream-sated cat as sensations rocked through her body in waves.

Impatient for the taste of her, Harley caught the nipple between his teeth and swirled his tongue around and around, while he fought the snaps free on his jeans.

"Oh, God, Harley," Mary Claire breathed, cupping his face between her hands, reveling in the feel of his jaw muscles working as he suckled. "That feels wonderful."

Her words of encouragement inflamed him. Her breast still in his mouth, he slipped his hand between her legs. She arched again at his touch, pressed her breast more fully against his face and at the same time opened for him. Wetting his finger in the molten honey, he traced the length of her feminine folds, his touch light and teasing, drawing her closer and closer to the fire.

Her hands dropped to his shoulders and her nails dug into his flesh. "Harley," she whispered desperately as she rocked her hips against his hand. But he kept his touch light, teasing her, refusing to give her what she wanted while he inched his jeans farther down his hips with his other hand. The swing rocked beneath him, mimicking their movements, adding an urgency to their lovemaking.

He felt the first tremors, felt the urgent drive of her hips against his hand and knew she was close. His breath burning in his lungs, his loins on fire with his need to satisfy them both, he lifted her, guiding her down until he rested against her flowered opening. He caught her hips in his hands and brought her fully against him. "Now, Mary Claire," he whispered hoarsely, "now!" Then he buried himself inside her.

Her back arched at the impact, her fingers digging into his shoulders. She gasped his name as he spilled into her, mingling his juices with hers. Her head drooped, her chin resting on the top of his head as she sucked in air. The tension slowly eased from her body.

"I think I can sleep now," she said, her breathy sigh blowing warm and fast against his brow as she brought her lips to his. "How about you?"

Seven

Stephie clapped her hands, jumping up and down. "Can I ride him?" she cried, looking from the pony to Harley, her eyes filled with an endearing mixture of excitement and hope.

Grinning, Harley swung a leg over the back of his saddle. The last time he'd promised Stephie a ride, the rattlesnake had spooked the pony so badly Harley hadn't thought it safe to put the child on his back. But Harley was a man who kept his promises. "That's why I brought him."

Stephie inched closer, holding out her hand to the pony that stood patiently beside Harley's horse. She laughed delightedly when the pony's velvet nose nudged her palm. "He likes me," she cried, her eyes wide with awe as she looked up at Harley.

Harley chuckled and unwrapped the lead rope from

his saddle's horn. "'Course he does. What's not to like?''

He tethered his own horse at the gate and scooped Stephie up in one arm. "Are you ready, cowgirl?''

"You bet!''

Harley swung her onto the saddle. "You hold on to the horn there while I lead him around a bit. After you get the hang of it, I'll let you give him a turn on your own.''

Her face wreathed in a smile, Stephie nodded.

"Our first stop, though, is the back door,'' he warned. "So we can make sure this is all right with your mother.''

Stephie nodded again and gripped the saddle horn tightly. Harley led her across the yard.

Mary Claire must have been at the sink washing dishes and seen them coming, because before Harley could announce their arrival, she was pushing through the screen door, drying her hands with a towel. She smiled at Stephie, then shifted her gaze to Harley's, her eyes taking on that smoky green hue he'd seen when they made love. "Good morning, Harley,'' she said, her husky voice stirring his blood to life.

What her voice didn't accomplish, the sight of her standing in the bright morning sunshine did. "Mornin', Mary Claire,'' he said, dragging off his hat, drinking in the sight of her and wishing with all his heart they could be alone. But that was impossible, at least for the moment. He nodded toward the pony. "I was wonderin' if you'd mind if I led Stephie around for a bit.''

Mary Claire folded her arms beneath her breasts,

chuckling. "A little late to be asking, don't you think?"

Harley had the grace to blush. "I can still pull her off. All you have to do is give the word."

Mary Claire quickly shook her head. "And break her heart? No. She can ride."

He nodded. "Well, we'll just take a stroll around the backyard and down the driveway a bit to test her handling. You gonna be around when we get back?"

Her smile warmed him all the way to his toes. "I'll be here," she promised softly.

With a nod, he grinned and backed away from the steps, then turned and led the pony across the backyard.

As she watched them, Mary Claire caught the towel she held to her breasts and sighed. She hadn't thought she'd ever fall in love again. Not after what Pete had put her through. But the feelings she had for Harley were growing by the day. And if it wasn't love she felt for him, it was darn close.

And that was what frightened her. She wasn't sure she was ready to trust a man with her heart again.

Sinking onto the top porch step, she watched as Harley murmured instructions to Stephie and noted the concentration with which her daughter listened. Harley was good to her children and good *for* them, and they both respected and liked him, which in Mary Claire's book was important. He'd make a wonderful father. She didn't doubt that for a minute.

She remembered well his panic when he'd thought Stephie and Jimmy had been abducted by their father. She remembered, too, what he'd said when she had told him the children would return on Sunday. He'd said he supposed *we* can survive that long without them, including himself right along with Mary Claire in missing them. If that didn't demonstrate his love for her children, she didn't know what else could.

Tucking her hand beneath her chin, she watched them circle and head back her way, enjoying the simple pleasure of watching him move. Tall and broad-shouldered, he walked with a slow easy gait, his boots kicking up dust with each step. He kept his head tipped toward Stephie, one hand on her leg, offering equal doses of encouragement and direction as she worked with the reins. But occasionally his gaze drifted toward the porch steps, and Mary Claire felt heat sear through her. They'd been lovers for almost a week now, yet a simple look from him was enough to make her go all warm inside.

When Harley had led the pony in a full circle, he returned to the porch. With a hand on the clip of the lead rope, he asked Stephie, "Think you can handle him now?"

Her face flushed with excitement, she gave a quick nod.

"Remember," he warned, "you're the boss. Pull on the right rein to turn right, the left to go left and pull back gently, saying, 'Whoa,' when you want him to stop."

"I remember," she replied, anxious to be on her own.

His fingers snapped on the clip, releasing the lead rope. "Okay, cowgirl. He's all yours."

Though Mary Claire's nerves jumped at the thought of her daughter being in sole control of the pony, she bit her tongue. Harley knew what he was doing and would do nothing that could bring Stephie harm.

Dropping down on the step next to Mary Claire, Harley laid a hand on her knee, letting his elbow drop intimately between her thighs. Together they watched as Stephie slowly turned the pony, then headed back the way she'd just come. "She's a natural," he said, smiling proudly.

"I don't know about being a natural, but she's certainly having a good time," Mary Claire replied, her gaze wistful as she watched Stephie ride away. She covered Harley's hand with hers and squeezed. "I remember when I was a little girl and dreamed of having a horse. Every Christmas I would ask Santa for one, then Christmas morning I'd run to my bedroom window and look outside, and cry when I discovered the backyard empty."

Harley twisted his head to look at her, his eyes full of sympathy for the girl and her dreams. "I'm sorry."

Mary Claire laughed, ruffling his hair as she tipped her nose to his and stole a quick kiss. "Don't be. Santa made the right decision. A backyard in a city like Houston is hardly the place to keep a horse."

Harley nodded sagely, then pursed his lips and gestured at Stephie. "Well, she's got one for as long as she wants him. You can keep him here or over at my place, doesn't matter. When she wants to ride, all she has to do is give me a holler."

"And her mother?" Mary Claire asked softly, pressing her shoulder against his. "What if she wants something?"

Harley whipped his gaze back to her and his heart tilted at what he saw in her eyes. He grinned, squeez-

ing her thigh against his. "I'd guess that would de-
pend on what that something is."

Harley sat before the long bar at the End of the
Road, letting the condensation from the beer mug he
held cool his hot hands. It wasn't the sun's heat he'd
hoped to escape that afternoon by dropping into
Hank's bar for a beer. It was Mary Claire. All he had
to do was think of her and his entire body turned into
a damn furnace. And satisfying that heat was becom-
ing a problem with the kids around all the time.

He loved her kids, both of them, but finding time
alone with Mary Claire to steal even a little kiss, was
almost impossible. On a frustrated sigh, he lifted the
mug and let the cold beer slide down his parched
throat.

Drying glasses not four feet away, Hank heard the
sigh and glanced Harley's way. "Missed you last Friday night."

Harley winced. He'd been so wrapped up in Mary
Claire, he hadn't even thought about the poker game
he regularly participated in on the first Friday night
of every month at Hank's bar. "I had a sick cow,"
he mumbled.

Hank arched a brow and bit back a smile, knowing
his friend well enough to recognize a lie when he
heard it. "Figured as much." Lazily, he polished the
glass. "Me and Cody considered driving out to your
place to check on you—"

Harley's heart jerked to a stop, then kicked back
into a nervous pounding against the wall of his chest.
He knew damn good and well that if they'd driven
out to his place, Cody and Hank would have found

him in bed with Mary Claire. Why that thought bothered him, he didn't know, because that was exactly where he wanted to be right now—at home in bed with Mary Claire.

"—but we figured you had everything under control," Hank finished.

The laughter in Hank's eyes was hard to miss, making Harley scowl. "I'm used to going it alone," he muttered.

Hank nodded and set down one glass to pick up another. "Saw you in town yesterday with that Reynolds woman and her kids."

Harley felt heat rise in his cheeks. His relationship with Mary Claire was too new and too special to share. "She needed my truck to haul some things to her place that wouldn't fit in that minivan of hers."

Hank's hand stilled on the glass, his eyes opening wide. "Why, that's right neighborly of you, Harley. Helping out a single woman that way." He chuckled and went back to his polishing. "But if she's ever in need of something a little more intimate than the loan of a truck, you just tell her to give old Hank here a call. I'd be more than willing to, uh, service her needs, so to speak."

Harley was stretched over the bar, his hand cinched tight around the collar of Hank's shirt before he even thought about what he was doing. "Don't you ever go near her, you hear me?" Harley ground out between clenched teeth. "If you do, I swear, I'll smash in your face."

Hank held out his hands in surrender. "Hey, buddy. I didn't know. You should've told me you'd already staked a claim."

Growling, Harley gave Hank a shove, sending him crashing into a shelf filled with liquor bottles. Then he wheeled and stomped from the bar. As he pushed through the door, he bumped into Cody.

"Hey, Harley! How you doin'?"

Ignoring the greeting, Harley pushed past Cody, muttering curses under his breath.

Cody stared after him. He watched him jump into his truck, then spew gravel as he spun onto the road. With a shrug he pulled open the door and entered the bar. "What's the matter with him?" he asked Hank, hooking a thumb over his shoulder.

Hank wagged his head soulfully as he plucked a mug from the rack to fill for Cody. "Seems you were right about Harley and that Reynolds woman." He sat the beer in front of the sheriff, then rested his forearms on the edge of the bar, looking as forlorn as if he'd just lost his best friend. "The man's got it bad," he muttered miserably.

Harley floored the accelerator, shooting down the county road to his house. He slapped the steering wheel with the heel of his hand and uttered a fervent "Damn!" Why had he handled Hank in such a way? Hank was his friend, for God's sake! And it wasn't like he'd never heard similar comments from him before. Hank was a born lady's man, a rounder constantly on the prowl for a woman who was of the same mind. And finding a willing woman had never been a hardship for Hank. With his movie-star looks, his easy smile and his black heart, he'd charmed more than his fair share into bed.

And that was the problem. When Hank had said he

would be willing to "service" Mary Claire, Harley had gone a little crazy at the idea of the two of them together. The thought of Mary Claire Reynolds in anybody's bed but his own sent his blood pressure shooting sky-high.

You should've told me you'd already staked a claim.

Harley remembered Hank's words and felt a stab of guilt for not setting the man straight. He didn't have any claim on Mary Claire Reynolds. Granted, they were lovers, but he didn't own her. Neither of them had made any promises to the other. They were just two lonely people who found comfort and pleasure in each other's company.

Harley wasn't looking to stake a claim. He didn't want another wife. He'd had one of those. And when she'd left him, he'd sealed off his heart, determined to never love again.

"We've got to quit meeting this way," Mary Claire groaned.

Harley's mouth creased into a grin against her cheek as he shifted her just a fraction on his lap. Still buried inside her, he put the toe of his boot against the porch's planked floor and eased the swing into motion beneath them, enjoying the feel of her around him. "And what's wrong with the way we meet?"

She groaned again and sat back and Harley felt himself slip from her warmth. "It's so...so...so frustrating," she finished, and curled a fist against his chest.

Purposely misunderstanding her, Harley circled her waist with his hands, drawing her hips full against him. "Well now, if you're still frustrated, we could give it another try," he offered.

In the moonlight Mary Claire saw the twinkle in his eye and smothered a laugh. "You are insatiable."

Harley leaned forward, catching the tip of the nipple that bobbed in front of his eyes. "So you've said," he murmured as he drew her breast into his mouth.

Framing his face with her hands, Mary Claire sighed. "What I meant," she said, then gave herself a moment to enjoy the sensations that flooded her at his tongue's teasing. "What I meant," she repeated, her breath growing short, "is that stolen moments aren't enough."

Harley slackened his hold on her waist and slowly released her nipple. With Hank's comment that afternoon still fresh in his mind, he was suddenly worried where this conversation was headed. "But...we've already discussed this," he said hesitantly. "It's like you said. The kids...well, it wouldn't be right for me to spend the night when they're around."

Shifting to sit across his lap, Mary Claire turned and laid her head against his shoulder. "I know. But it's still frustrating," she murmured, snuggling against his bare chest. "I want to go to sleep at night with you at my side and wake up with you in the morning and not be sneaking in and out of the house in the dark."

Harley remained silent.

She sighed heavily and curled an arm around his waist. "Hold me, Harley," she whispered. "Just hold me."

If his hold on her was a little hesitant and his body

a little tense, Mary Claire didn't seem to notice. She just sighed again, her eyelashes tickling the hair on his chest as she closed her eyes and cuddled closer against the warmth and strength of the man who held her.

Exhausted, Harley crawled into his bed, telling himself he wasn't going to see Mary Claire that night. He was too old to go chasing through the night all the time like some teenager with raging hormones. He was over forty, a rancher who rose before dawn and worked long and hard until past dusk. He was a man who needed his rest if he wanted to meet the grueling challenges of running a cattle ranch alone.

He groaned, pushing his fists against his eyes, knowing his age and his work was only an excuse, and a feeble one at that. The truth was he was scared. More scared than he'd ever been in his life. Mary Claire was starting to say things, little things, that led him to believe that she wanted something more permanent from him than the stolen hours of pleasure they managed to grab.

He narrowed his eyes at the ceiling, trying to recall her exact words from the night before. Something about going to sleep every night at his side and waking up with him every morning. Without realizing he was doing so, he pressed a hand over his heart. Damn, if he didn't want the same thing.

A woman, children, a home. Everything Harley had ever desired. But he'd trusted a woman once with his heart, and she had all but broken it when she'd left him, taking his kids with her. Groaning, he rolled to his side, drawing the pillow to his chest as he had so many times in the past, seeking comfort. Tonight he found little peace in the soft down, but instead, found himself longing for Mary Claire's warm body curved against his.

That he would desire a woman didn't surprise him. He was human, after all, and still breathing. That he would want one with such intensity, to the point where he thought of nothing but her throughout his day, shocked him. After Susan had left, he'd vowed never to love again. His fingers knotted in the pillow at the thought while fear twisted through his stomach. Love? Was that what he felt for Mary Claire?

A storm was brewing outside, as strong as the one that suddenly swept to life inside him. He listened to the wind pick up, howling around the corner of his stone house, rattling tree branches against its tin roof, and he felt its turbulence echo deep inside of him. Love. Damn, if that single, four-letter word didn't scare the hell out of him!

But scared or not, he knew he wanted to be with her, if to do nothing more than hold her.

On a sigh, Harley rolled to the edge of the bed and reached for his jeans.

The sky was pitch-black, and without stars or moon to light his way, Harley could see no farther than a foot or so beyond his horse's head. Thunder rumbled low in the distance and he lifted his nose, scenting the coming rain, knowing that when it came it would arrive with a vengeance.

Lightning ribboned a corner of the sky, still far enough away to pose no threat. Harley pressed his knees into his horse's sides, easing the animal into a trot. *I've got to be crazy,* he told himself. *Chasing across the countryside in the middle of the night like some lovesick teenager, and with a storm brewing, no less.*

He chuckled ruefully, the sound coming from low in his chest, echoing the distant rumble of thunder. Yeah, he was crazy all right. And the source of his madness, if she was smart, was fast asleep in her bed. A new bolt of lightning flashed, illuminating a ghostly figure standing at the pasture gate. A slow smile spread across his face as he realized it was Mary Claire. The wind caught the hem of her nightgown, whipping it around her legs. Harley urged his horse into a lope.

At the gate, he reined the horse to a stop and slid from the saddle. "What are you doin' out here?" he asked Mary Claire.

Smiling, she leaned across the gate and pulled his face to hers for a kiss. "Waiting for you," she said breathlessly as the wind whipped her hair around her face. She quickly unhooked the gate and held it open while Harley led his horse through. After refastening it she fell into step beside him, looping her arm through his and hugging it to her. "I was afraid you wouldn't come because of the storm."

"Oh, I would've made it all right," he replied, knowing in his heart it was true. "Even if I'd had to build an ark and sail over."

Laughing, Mary Claire rose on tiptoe and pressed a kiss to his cheek.

Harley dragged his arm from hers and slung it across her shoulders, pulling her against his side. "Would you mind if I put my horse in that old shed by the garage? It'll keep him dry when the rain starts."

"No, I don't mind."

Together they crossed to the shed, quickly unsaddled the horse and settled him inside, then headed for the front porch. Just as they reached the steps, the sky opened up, dumping thick sheets of rain that rattled against the tin roof. They ducked under the porch, laughing, then fell into each other's arms while raindrops ran in rivulets down their faces.

"Oh, Harley," she murmured against his lips. "I was so afraid you wouldn't come."

"I couldn't stay away," he said, his voice husky. He caught her rain-dampened hair and scraped it back to look down into her face. Her beauty nearly blinded him, and he wondered, not for the first time, what she found attractive in an old rancher like him.

She shivered and he pulled her close again, one hand cupping the back of her neck. "You're soaked," he said, feeling her shiver. "You need to go inside and get on dry clothes and get under the covers."

She tipped her head to look up at him. "Only if you'll come with me," she whispered.

Lightning flashed, and in that split second of illumination, just before the crash of thunder, Harley saw the urgency, the utter seriousness in her eyes.

"Are you sure?" he asked.

She took his hand in hers, pulling him behind her. "Yes, I'm sure."

The screen door opened with a slight squeak and Harley held his breath, hesitating, but followed when Mary Claire gave his hand a gentle tug. They climbed the stairs, both tiptoeing, trying to keep their steps light. At the top of the stairs, Mary Claire turned and ducked into her bedroom with Harley close behind.

Lightning streaked outside the window, seeming to light the entire sky. The thunder cracked again, shaking the old house. A soft whimper filtered down the hallway and through the door and Harley froze.

"It's okay," Mary Claire assured him in a low whisper. "It's just Stephie. I'll check on her while you get out of those wet clothes."

Harley found himself alone in the room, but the scent of her remained. He inhaled deeply, filling himself with the fragrance that was so much a part of Mary Claire.

He moved quietly to the dresser and picked up a picture. Squinting against the darkness, he could just make out the faces of Mary Claire, Stephie and Jimmy smiling at him from the center of a pewter frame. A Christmas tree served as their background.

His heart stirred as he wondered what it would be like to share Christmas with them. Waking up Christmas morning with Mary Claire at his side. Watching the kids rip through a pile of brightly wrapped gifts. Eating a late breakfast, then settling back on the couch with Mary Claire to watch the kids play with their new toys. He sighed as he replaced the frame, suddenly acutely aware of the depth of his feelings for each person pictured there. When had it happened? he asked himself. When had he opened up his heart and let this woman and her children inside?

Slowly, he moved back to the bed and began to work the buttons of his shirt free. When he was naked, his damp clothes in a pile by the side of the bed, he stripped back the covers and eased himself be-

tween the sheets. Arranging the pillows behind his
head, he settled back to wait.

He heard Mary Claire's soft footsteps in the hallway, then saw her slip into the room and pause to
close the door behind her. Crossing to the opposite
side of the bed, she lifted her nightgown over her
head, then dropped it and slipped into bed beside him.
Shivering, she tucked her head in the curve of his
shoulder and placed her hand over his heart. He covered it with his own.

"Is she okay?" he whispered.

He felt her nod against his chest. "She's fine.
Didn't even wake up. She was just moaning in her
sleep."

He sighed and hugged her close.

She tipped her face to his, finding his lips with hers
in the darkness. "Oh, Harley," she said on a long,
shuddery breath, and snuggled against his chest.

With nothing on his mind but holding her, he
brought his hand up her arm and cupped a breast. The
ball of his thumb moved lazily across the nipple. He
felt it tighten and bud into a hard knot at his lazy
teasing while rain pounded against the window. It
echoed the pounding growing inside him. Sliding
down the pillows propped at his back, he hauled Mary
Claire across his front.

He kissed her with the fierceness of the storm that
raged outside until she was breathless and squirming
against him. Sliding farther down the pillow, he
caught a budded nipple between his teeth, then closed
his mouth over her breast while catching the other
nipple between his thumb and forefinger, mimicking
his tongue's teasing on the opposite breast.

Braced above him with her hands on either side of his head, she whimpered, dipping her head over his until her damp hair curtained his face, bringing to him the scent of rain. With each lave of his tongue, she ground her hips harder against his in a frantic search for release from the demons he'd unleashed inside her. Moving his hands to span her waist, he guided her to him, then slipped his fingers between her legs to spread her feminine lips.

At the first thrust, she bucked beneath him and he heard her sharp intake of breath. Quickly, he covered her mouth with his to stifle her cry. With her mouth pressed hard against his, she rode him, each slap of her flesh against his, an echo of the rain pounding on the tin roof overhead. Lightning flashed and thunder rolled, and she jerked her lips from his, arching her back as the storm drove her on and on.

Gathering her hair in a tangled wad, she threw back her head and arched again, taking him more fully inside her, then deeper still. A clap of thunder crashed against the house and Mary Claire seemed to explode right along with it. Unable to hold back any longer, Harley caught her hips in his hands and filled her with his seed.

Lightning ripped through the darkness outside the window, and in its illumination Harley watched Mary Claire's face grow slack, her body soften and her hands trail seductively down her body until they lay on his chest. Slowly she wilted against him and he held her while the storm raged on through the night.

Harley awoke before dawn, as was his habit, and snuggled closer to Mary Claire's back, smiling sleepily when she sighed and curled her hips against his groin. The rain, though softer now, continued to patter against the tin roof. He knew he had to go before the kids woke up. Explaining his presence in their mother's bed was a chore he didn't want to take on—at least not yet.

He pushed himself up on an elbow and, lifting her hair from her cheek, placed a kiss there. She mewled softly in her sleep, and burrowed closer. Grinning, he slipped from the bed and snugged the covers around her to keep her warm. Though he would rather have crawled back into bed with her, he forced himself to pull on his clothes, knowing that even though it was still raining, he had work to do.

He grabbed his boots and tiptoed across the room in his stocking feet, opening the door slowly, then slipping through. He paused with his hand on the doorknob and glanced back to the bed where Mary Claire slept—and knew it was where he wanted to be. Not just now, but forever.

While the rain continued to sluice down the window behind her, Mary Claire sat at her desk, frowning at Harley's ledger, spread in front of her. An asset she hadn't paid much attention to before drew the frown—a bank account set up in the name of R. M. Kerr. Puzzled, she shifted through the stack of bank statements until she found one labeled with the same name. She pulled the sheets from the envelope.

The name at the top was the same as that on the ledger—R. M. Kerr—and she quickly verified that the account number matched, as well. Her frown deepening, she studied the quarterly statement. Four deposits, no withdrawals and a balance that nearly stole Mary Claire's breath. *What is this?* she wondered. And more importantly, *who* is this?

Scrambling through the pile of statements from the previous year, she pulled the ones for the account and spread them in front of her. Each was exactly the same. Four deposits, no withdrawals, an interest payment with each new total, showing a steadily increasing balance.

Had he established the savings account for his children? she wondered, then quickly shoved aside that notion. She'd already found accounts for both his children, probably money he was setting aside for Jenny and Tommy's college educations.

So who is R. M. Kerr? she asked herself again.

The telephone rang and she reached for it, her thoughts still focused on the bank statement she held in her other hand.

"Hello?" she said absently.

"Hi, Mary Claire!"

At the sound of her friend Leighanna's voice, Mary Claire dropped the statement and sank back in her chair, a smile of pleasure curving at her mouth. "Leighanna! It's wonderful to hear your voice!"

"Yours, too. We've been so worried, and when neither Reggie nor I had heard from you, we decided we'd better check up on you."

"Is Reggie there?"

"No, she's showing an apartment. You know Reggie. Work, work, work."

Mary Claire laughed, thinking of her friend who

was also the owner of the apartment complex where she'd lived in Houston. "Yes, that's our Reggie."

"She sends her love, though," Leighanna added.

"Give her mine, too."

"So how are you doing?"

"Fine. No, better than fine," she quickly amended. "Great! The house is looking more and more like home, and the kids are loving it here."

"You sound happy."

Mary Claire smiled at the relief she heard in Leighanna's voice. "I am." She caught her lower lip between her teeth, knowing that Harley was a large part of that happiness and wondering if she should mention him to Leighanna. "I've met someone," she said hesitantly, and nearly laughed again when she heard Leighanna's shocked intake of breath.

"You have?"

"Yes, and he's wonderful."

"Oh, Mary Claire! I can't believe I'm hearing this. Who is he?"

"A neighbor. A rancher. And the kindest, most gentle man I've ever known."

"And?" Leighanna prodded.

Mary Claire rested her head on the back of the chair, remembering last night and sighing. "And, yes, he's a great lover."

"Jeez, Mary Claire, you don't waste any time. Is this serious?"

Mary Claire's forehead pleated in a slight frown as she considered the question. "Yes, I think it is," she replied softly.

"When do we get to meet him?"

"Whenever you like."

"I thought I might come, not this weekend but the next, if that's all right."

"Of course it is! Will Reggie be coming with you?"

"No. You know Reggie. She thinks her real-estate office will fall apart if she isn't there to keep things going smoothly."

Mary Claire sighed. It was Reggie's one fault. She was a workaholic. Between her real-estate office and the apartment complex she owned, she worked long hours and rarely took time off. Of the three of them, Reggie was the most financially secure, yet it had always surprised Mary Claire that Reggie continued to live in one of the apartments at the complex she owned, when she could well afford to move to a much nicer place.

"Yes, I know," Mary Claire said sadly. "But if you can convince her to tear herself away from her work, please tell her that she's welcome to come, too. I'd love to see you both."

"Speaking of work, have you found a job yet?"

"Sort of. I've started a bookkeeping business working out of my home. This way I can still be here with Stephie and Jimmy."

"Mary Claire, that's fantastic!"

"Don't get too excited. It's small yet. In fact, I only have one client, but I hope the ad I ran in last week's paper will generate more business."

"Why didn't you ever think to do this in Houston? You wouldn't have ever had to move."

Mary Claire's eyes widened at the suggestion. "Well, I don't know," she said slowly. "I guess I just never thought of it."

"Well, it's not too late. You can always come back home."

"Move back to Houston?" Mary Claire said in surprise.

"Yes! Just think of all the business you could find here compared to Temptation. Houston's a gold mine of opportunity."

A movement in the doorway caught Mary Claire's eye, and she glanced up to see Harley standing in the doorway, a frown gathered between his brows. He had a folder tucked under his arm. "I'll give it some thought, but I've got to run now," she said into the receiver, and winked at Harley. "My client just arrived."

"Oh, darn. Well, I'll see you in a couple of weeks. You can give me all the details on this romance of yours then. Love you, Mary Claire."

"I love you, too."

She replaced the receiver. "A friend from Houston," she said by way of explanation, then rocked back in her chair. "What have you got?" she asked, nodding at the folder tucked under his arm.

Still frowning, Harley stepped into the office and dropped the folder on her desk. "These are the bills that came in this week, along with a few invoices for feed and the like. I thought you might need them."

She stretched and pulled the folder to her, flipping it open. "Yes, I do," she said, quickly thumbing through the envelopes and paper inside before looking back up at him. It was then she realized he still wore the frown. "Is something wrong?" she asked in concern.

If possible, his frown deepened. "No. Why?"

She laughed, tapping her finger to her own forehead. "You could plant a crop in those furrows on your forehead."

He shook his head, absently rubbing a hand across the creases. "I've just got a lot on my mind."

Knowing that the rain must cause him extra work, she nodded in sympathy. "Well, I'm glad you stopped by. I need to ask you something." She closed the folder and, pulling the bank statement from beneath it, spun it around for Harley to see. "What's this?"

Harley leaned over the desk to look, and his frown returned. "That's a savings account," he mumbled.

"I can see that," she said dryly. "But who is R. M. Kerr?"

"My sister." At the look of surprise on her face, he added, "My stepsister."

"You never mentioned a stepsister before."

He shoved his hands in his pockets. "Never came up."

"Well, where is she? And why do you keep her savings account?"

"I don't know where she is. She ran away over ten years ago. Haven't heard a word from her since."

Ten years may have passed, but Mary Claire could hear the pain in his voice and knew that her leaving had left a scar. "And this account?" she prodded, pointing to the statement.

"It's her share of the farm's profits."

Mary Claire's eyes widened in surprise. "You mean you've been socking away her profits all these years and you don't have a clue where she is?"

Harley lifted one shoulder in a shrug. "The money's rightfully hers. There's always the chance she might come home and claim it.''

Mary Claire just shook her head, marveling at the fairness and generosity in this man she loved. It was a part of his character she was sure he didn't even realize was there. Pushing to her feet, she planted her palms on the desk and leaned across it. "Come here," she ordered gently.

Hesitating slightly, Harley stepped to the edge of the desk, his scowl deepening. "What?"

"Closer," she said.

He leaned over and she caught his ears, drawing his face to hers until their noses bumped. "You are, undoubtedly, the kindest, fairest, most generous man I've ever known." She pressed her lips to his.

He responded immediately, grabbing her elbows and deepening the kiss, his mouth bruising, almost punishing hers. Then just as quickly, he released her and spun away, turning his back to her. Stunned by the anger she'd tasted in him, Mary Claire could only stare.

"Harley, what's wrong?"

His back to her, his hands on his hips, he shook his head. "Nothing's wrong."

But Mary Claire sensed something was very wrong. But what, she couldn't fathom. She came around the desk and stood behind him, laying a gentle hand on his shoulder. "Harley?"

He took a step away and her hand slipped from his shoulder. "I'm going to be out of town this weekend," he said curtly. "I'm going to San Antonio to see my kids."

"All right," she murmured, wondering why he had

waited until now to tell her this. "When will you be back?"

"Sunday. Probably late." He turned slowly and met her gaze. Mary Claire nearly wilted at the coolness of his expression. "I'll ask Cody to keep an eye on my place," he said, averting his gaze again. "If anything comes up, you can call him."

And then he was gone. Mary Claire listened to the front door close behind him and felt the first stab of fear.

Eight

"Oh, Dad, I wish you'd called before you came."

Harley sank onto the bed in his hotel room in San Antonio, his heart sinking. "I know, Jenny. But the decision to come for a visit was sort of spur-of-the-moment."

"Tommy left this morning to spend the weekend with some of his friends at Texas A&M University, and I'm leaving in a few minutes to go to a Spurs game with a bunch of my friends. We're all spending the night at Rachel's afterward."

Harley spread his hand across his face, squeezing at his temples, then dragged his fingers to his eyes and pressed. "That's okay, honey," he said, trying to mask the disappointment in his voice. "I understand." He looked up at the ceiling and blinked back tears. "How about tomorrow? Got any free time then?"

"Well..." Jenny replied hesitantly, "we'll probably sleep late. You know how slumber parties are."

No, Harley didn't know, which made his heart contract even more.

He heard her sigh. "And tomorrow afternoon we'd
all planned on going shopping at the mall. I guess we
could have dinner together afterward, if you want to
hang around that long."

The idea of sitting around a hotel room all day
didn't sound too inviting, but the alternative was going back home—and he wasn't ready to do that yet.
If possible, the pain there outweighed the disappointment he was experiencing at the moment.

"Dinner sounds fine," he said.

The auctioneer's chant rose above the sounds of
the crowd that had gathered for the auction. Horses,
from the regal Arabian to the lowly mule, kicked up
dust to thicken the air in the cavernous barn. Harley
found an empty seat and slipped into it.

The auctioneer conducted the bidding from a raised
platform in the center of the ring. Harley hadn't come
to buy anything, but he sat through more than an hour
of heavy bidding, watching as different breeds of
horses were led one by one into the ring. Though his
gaze remained fixed on the action, his mind was a
hundred miles away—in Temptation. More specifi-
cally, on Mary Claire. Playing back over and over
again the telephone conversation he'd overheard Friday morning. And he could see it happening all over
again. Losing those he loved to the pull of the big
city.

He sighed and shifted on the metal bleacher, unconsciously pressing a hand to his heart, trying to ease the pain there. The images built, anyway, squeezing their way through his chest and climbing higher until they filled his mind with memories. Mary Claire. Jimmy. Precious little Stephie.

He shook his head, trying to dispel the images. He couldn't go through that again, he told himself. Not now. Not ever. After Susan had left, he'd thought he'd go crazy. To survive, he'd steeled himself against ever falling in love again. But somehow, over the weeks, Mary Claire and her kids had slipped past his defenses and settled themselves in his heart and in his life.

But it wasn't too late, he told himself. He'd cut his losses and get on with just surviving as he'd done before. He could do it. He knew he could. The alternative was too bleak to consider.

"And get a look at this little mare," the auctioneer called.

Harley forced himself to focus on the sorrel mare being led into the arena. Head held high, she pranced nervously into the arena, her mane and tail flying like banners in the wind. The handler halted her in the center of the ring just beneath the auctioneer's platform. She danced around him, fighting his hold on the lead rope, her eyes wild with fear. Harley remembered witnessing a similar look in Mary Claire's eyes that first day he'd met her in Temptation—when she'd jumped him, thinking he meant to harm her kids.

In an effort to block the memory, he forced himself to concentrate on the mare. She was a beautiful animal, well formed, full of spirit. Her coat was slick and glossy—and so close to the color of Mary

Claire's hair that Harley found himself fisting his hands against his thighs.

I remember when I was a little girl and dreamed of having a horse. Every Christmas I would ask Santa for one, then Christmas morning I'd run to my bedroom window and look outside, and cry when I discovered the backyard empty.

The sound of Mary Claire's voice, wistful with the unrealized dreams of the little girl she had been, played through Harley's mind.

"And what'll you give me?" the auctioneer cried, beginning his chant.

The mare turned her head and looked straight at Harley. Without even thinking, Harley pulled the numbered card from his shirt pocket and lifted it.

"I've got a thousand, who'll give me two, who'll give me two?"

The bidding went on until only Harley and a man in the front row of the bleachers remained. Every time the man lifted his card, Harley shot his up in the air. Finally the man turned and met Harley's gaze. They stared long and hard at each other, with Harley's gaze never once wavering. With a frustrated shake of his head, the man finally turned back around and stuffed his card into his shirt pocket.

Harley had bought himself a mare.

The rain continued throughout the weekend, keeping Mary Claire and the kids in the house. She was sure that Harley would call her, that she'd misread his dark mood, his reserve, but she was disappointed when the phone didn't ring even once. The kids, of course, missed him and asked about his whereabouts.

She simply told them he had gone to visit his children and kept her fears to herself.

Cody came by to check on Harley's cows in Mary Claire's pasture on both Saturday and Sunday. Mary Claire watched him slog through the mud at the gate from her kitchen window Sunday morning. She had worked herself into such a frenzy, worrying about Harley and his odd behavior, that she decided to talk to Cody to see if Harley had said anything to him before he left. Grabbing a rain slicker from the rack at the back door, she pushed through the screen door and waited on the back porch for his return.

When he strode back to his truck after closing the gate, she darted from beneath the overhang and across the yard, waving her hand over her head. "Cody!" she called as she ran. "Wait up!"

He stopped and glanced her way. Rain dripped steadily from the plastic covering over his straw cowboy hat. "Mary Claire, what are you doing out in this mess?"

She stopped in front of him, her body suddenly nothing but a knot of raw nerves and her questions lodged tight in her throat. How could she ask this man, this virtual stranger, if Harley had shared anything that might concern her?

Rain stung her face as she looked up at him, but when she found nothing but kindness in his eyes, she swallowed back her fears. "When Harley left, he seemed upset about something. I just wondered if maybe he'd said anything to you about...well, about me or why he was upset."

Cody frowned. "No, ma'am. He didn't say much of anything. Just asked if I'd check on his cattle while he was out of town. He did say he was going to see his kids in San Antonio.''

Mary Claire's shoulders drooped in disappointment. ''Yes, he told me that much. But he just seemed so...distant when he left. I've been worried.''

Cody laid a comforting hand on her shoulder. ''I wouldn't worry that pretty head of yours over this. Harley's a man who keeps everything pretty much inside. His mood might have been nothing more than him missing his kids.''

Mary Claire nodded. ''You're probably right.'' She forced a smile. ''Thanks, Cody.''

''No thanks needed.'' He turned her around and gave her a gentle shove. ''Now get on back to the house before you drown.''

Mary Claire ran to the house, waving to him over her shoulder. But she couldn't let go of her worries. They plagued her long after the children went to bed that night. She sat at her window dressed in her nightgown, watching the rain sluice down the glass as she waited for Harley, sure that he would come as he had so many times before, under the cover of darkness. When the mantel clock downstairs struck two, she dragged herself wearily from the window and crawled into bed.

He wasn't coming. Not tonight, nor tomorrow night. Something inside told her he would never be coming again.

Mary Claire put on a brave face for the children over the next week, telling them when they asked about Harley that she was sure he was just too busy to come for a visit. Being away for an entire weekend, he would have a lot of work to catch up on. But when the next weekend arrived, and he still hadn't appeared, she could see they no longer bought her story. Jimmy simply quit asking, but Mary Claire would catch him looking at her in a sympathetic way.

Stephie, though, was a different story. She begged Mary Claire to call Harley, even cried when Mary Claire refused. She sulked around the house, her small face the picture of dejection, until Mary Claire was tempted to cry herself.

She did cry. But only at night in the privacy of her room. Lying on her bed, with her knees pulled to her chest, she soaked her pillow with her tears, longing for the man she'd foolishly given her heart to and wondering what had gone wrong.

Mary Claire heard the rattle of an old car on the drive and quickly dropped her dishcloth to run outside. A smile spread across her face as she watched Leighanna step from her battered Chevy. She flew down the steps, her arms outstretched.

"You made it!" she cried, hugging Leighanna to her, then holding her at arm's length so she could look at her. "I worried that your rattletrap of a car wouldn't make the long drive."

Leighanna groaned. "Me, too." She lifted her damp blond hair from her neck. "The air conditioner quit on me about halfway here."

Mary Claire shook her head in sympathy. "Poor thing. You're probably dying of thirst." Linking Leighanna's arm in hers, she headed for the house. "I just made a fresh pitcher of iced tea."

Leighanna moaned. "Oh, that sounds like heaven."

Jimmy met them in kitchen. "Hi, Leighanna!" he said with a welcoming grin, then ducked when she tried to give him a hug.

Leighanna laughed and ruffled his hair. "Oh, it won't be long before you'll be clamoring for a woman's hugs."

Jimmy rolled his eyes. "Yeah, right."

Mary Claire chuckled, then spun her son around and gave his rear end a swat. "Go and tell Stephie Leighanna's here." She gestured for Leighanna to take a seat at the table as she poured the tea. "Lemon or sugar?"

"Both, please. I need all the sustenance I can get."

Mary Claire chuckled again and dropped a lemon slice into the glass. Placing the tea and a spoon in front of her friend, she dropped into the chair opposite hers, then shoved the sugar bowl Leighanna's way.

Leighanna added a generous spoonful to the tea and stirred. "Well? Where is he?"

Mary Claire's heart stopped for an instant, painfully aware who Leighanna meant. "Well," she replied hesitantly, "he's gone. Not gone, really," she clarified at Leighanna's startled look. "He just doesn't come around anymore."

Leighanna set the spoon down. "But I thought..."

Mary Claire's eyes filled with unexpected tears. "Me, too."

"Mom?"

She swiped at the tears and turned to find Jimmy standing in the doorway. "What, son?"

"I can't find Stephie."

Mary Claire frowned. "Did you look in her room?"

"Yeah. I even went outside. She's not anywhere."

Mary Claire jumped to her feet, knocking over the chair, her heart rocketing to her throat. "But she has to be somewhere!" she cried.

Jimmy lifted his hands in a shrug. "I've looked everywhere."

Mary Claire tried to think where Stephie might go. "Harley," she said, the name coming out on a rush of breath.

"What?" Leighanna asked.

Mary Claire brought her gaze to her friend's. "Harley. Our neighbor. She's been miserable because he hasn't been coming around. I'll bet she's gone to his house to see him." She ran for the counter and grabbed her keys. "Would you stay with Jimmy?" she asked. "I'll be back as quick as I can."

Leighanna urged her out the back door. "Of course I will. You just make sure Stephie's all right."

Harley backed the tractor into position and pushed the hydraulic lever that lowered the round bale of hay into place. Cattle surged around the bale, bawling. The rain had turned the pasture into one huge mud hole, and with the extra herd of cattle he'd moved there to keep them away from the rain-swollen creek, he'd been forced to put out hay to prevent them from stripping the field bare of grass. Harley frowned at the deep tracks the tractor had cut. It would take days for the ground to dry out enough to plow it smooth again.

Though enclosed in the tractor's cab, he thought he

heard a horn honk. He glanced up to peer through the windshield and saw Mary Claire's van driving down the lane at breakneck speed.

"What the hell?" he muttered as he watched her wheel to a stop at the fence opposite him. She jumped from the van, waving her arms over her head. Realizing something was wrong, Harley jerked the tractor free of the bale of hay, thrust it into gear and spun through the mud in the direction of the fence.

As he neared, he saw the tears on Mary Claire's face and the frantic way she twisted her hands. He stomped on the brake and leapt from the tractor. "What's wrong?" he cried as he vaulted over the fence.

"It's Stephie," Mary Claire sobbed. "She's gone."

"Gone?" Harley grabbed Mary Claire's shoulders and shook her. "Where? Where's she gone?"

Angrily Mary Claire wrenched from his grasp. "I don't know!" she cried. "I thought she was with you."

Harley looked confused. "With me? I haven't seen her."

Mary Claire fisted her hands at her sides, her eyes blazing with anger. "It's all your fault!" she screamed, then swung a fist at his chest.

Harley took a step back. "My fault?" he asked in amazement.

"Yes, yours! She's been miserable all week because you don't come and see her anymore." Her shoulders trembled as she glared at him accusingly. "You made us love you, all of us, then as soon as you got what you wanted from me, you dumped us."

She pummeled his chest with her fists. "It's your fault! All your fault she's run away!"

Harley caught her fists in his hands. "Mary Claire, stop it!" he ordered sternly. "This isn't helping find Stephie."

The fight sagged out of her and the tears returned, streaming down her cheeks. She tugged her hands from his grasp and covered her face, letting the tears flow.

Harley fought the urge to gather her into his arms. "Have you called Cody?"

She shook her head, dragging her hands from her face. "I was so sure she'd be here with you."

Harley thought of the acres and acres of land that stretched between the two houses and the dangers they held. There were several abandoned wells she might have fallen into, rattlesnakes, a swollen creek. Harley's stomach knotted in dread.

He caught Mary Claire by the elbow and headed her back to the van. "Go home and call Cody. Tell him to get a search party together." He squinted up at the sun. "We've only got another couple of hours of daylight left," he said almost to himself. He turned back to Mary Claire, his lips pressed into a tight line. "I'll saddle my horse and start a search from this side. Tell Cody to meet me at the fence line where our properties meet."

Harley rode, his eyes scanning the ground, searching for any sign that Stephie had come this way. Occasionally he lifted his hands to cup his mouth and call her name. Each time he listened, praying he would hear her voice, find her safe. When he didn't, he urged his horse on, making a slow sweep from one side of the acreage to the other. He rode for more than an hour before he reached the fence line where Cody waited with four other men. They stood ready, as he knew they would be, their horses saddled and loaded with gear. Rifles, flashlights, blankets. They'd come prepared.

Harley gave Cody a tight-lipped greeting. "I've covered the center pasture, the one that stretches back to my house. We'll need to break into two groups to search the rest. Hank, you and Charlie take the north pasture. Cody, you and Marvin take the south—it borders Jack Barlow's place. I'm going to follow the creek from here back to Mary Claire's. If any of you find Stephie, shoot your rifle once in the air."

Without waiting for their acknowledgment, he jerked the reins across his horse's neck and spun him around, then kicked him into a gallop toward the line of trees that followed the creek. Before he could even see it, he heard the creek's roar. The rain during the past week had brought the water level to near flood stage. Three of his cows had drowned trying to ford it. He felt a moment's panic, thinking of Stephie slipping and falling into the rushing water, her tiny body being dragged along by the swift current, no match for the strength of the swollen stream.

He cupped his hands around his mouth. "Stephie!" He waited, listening, holding his breath, praying silently he'd hear her call back—but he heard nothing but the rushing water. Urging the horse to the bank, he headed east toward Mary Claire's house, his gaze sweeping both banks. He rode for what seemed like hours, although he knew by the sun's descent behind him it couldn't have been more than one.

He stopped again and called her name, his voice hoarse now from all the hollering. "Ste-phie!" He stood up in the stirrups, and braced his hands on the saddle horn, listening intently for any sound. Desperate now, knowing that once the sun set, the chances of finding her alive would narrow, he urged his horse on.

A flash of blue on the opposite bank caught his eye. He reined his horse to a stop and swung down from the saddle. Water rushed around him as he waded waist-deep into the swollen creek. Twice he stumbled and nearly fell before he reached the tree branch that dipped into the churning water and the piece of cloth snagged there. He ripped the fabric from the branch and immediately recognized it as a piece of one of Stephie's favorite T-shirts.

Clutching it, he thrashed his way back through the water and to his horse. He grabbed the horn, swung himself up into the saddle and urged the horse on, calling Stephie's name until his throat was raw.

"Harley! Help me! I'm over here!"

He heard the weak voice and stopped, his gaze sweeping the far side of the creek. He saw her then, about a hundred feet ahead, partially obscured by the fallen tree she clung to.

"I'm coming, Stephie! Hold on!" He wove his way through the tangle of brush, then jumped to the ground and quickly untied the rope attached to his saddle. Stepping into the loop, he jerked it tight around his waist, then wrapped the opposite end around the saddle horn. He gathered the extra length of rope and coiled it in his hand. While murmuring instructions to his horse, he gave the rope a yank and the horse backed, drawing the hemp into a tight line.

Harley toed off his boots and waded into the water, only to discover, as he'd feared, that the water was well over his head here. Using one arm to swim with and the other to hold the coiled rope above the water, he eased out more length as needed. He swam until his arm ached with fatigue. When he was close enough, he made a grab for the tree that held Stephie, missed, then grabbed again. Getting a fistful of small branches in his hand, he gritted his teeth and pulled for all he was worth. Little by little, inch by inch, he worked through the mass of tangled branches until he was no more than a few feet from Stephie—and realized he was out of rope.

"Stephie? Are you okay?" he gasped, his breath tearing through his burning lungs.

"Yes," she sobbed. "But my arm hurts. I can't hold on...."

"Yes, you can," Harley said firmly. "Now I want you to try to kick your way toward me."

"No!" she cried. "I can't!"

He saw the fear in her eyes and sought to calm her. "Yes, you can. Just keep a good grip on that branch. I'm right here and I'm gonna catch you, okay?"

Her frightened eyes measured the short distance between them, and he could see that to her it seemed like a mile. "You can do it, sweetheart," he told her. "I know you can."

He watched her swallow, then slowly loosen the fingers of one hand while with the other she held the branch in a death grip. Tentatively, she turned toward him, her feet churning the water. Her little fingers reached out and though Harley stretched as far as he could, he couldn't quite grasp her.

Frustrated, he bit back a curse. "You can swim, can't you, Stephie?" he asked, keeping his voice calm.

"A little," came her quivering response.

"Good. Now I want you to let go of that tree and swim as hard as you can toward me and I'll catch you. On the count of three. Are you ready?"

She sniffled, but bravely nodded her head.

"One...two...three."

One by one, her white-knuckled fingers slipped from the tree, then her arms were slapping frantically at the water. But she was no match for the strong current. It caught her and began to carry her away from him. With a mighty lunge against the rope that dug into his waist, Harley grabbed for her, caught one of her hands and hung on. Fighting the current, he managed to pull her near enough to get a grip on her wrist. With his heart in his throat, he hauled her all the way to his chest.

Sobbing hysterically now, she wrapped her arms tight around his neck and clung.

"Now, now," he soothed, "no need to cry. You're safe. Harley's got you."

Her arms tightened around his neck and she buried her face against his shoulder. Harley caught the rope and gave it a sharp tug. "Back, boy," he shouted to his horse. "Back."

The big roan horse backed up while Harley pulled them to the bank and to safety.

Flanked by Cody and the other men from the search party, Harley rode through the gate with Stephie, wrapped snuggly in a blanket, on the saddle in front of him. He heard the slap of the back door as it hit the wall of the house and saw, through the growing dusk, Mary Claire streak across the yard toward them, her arms held out.

"Oh, Stephie, baby!" she cried, reaching up and pulling her from Harley's arms. "Are you okay?"

At the sight of her mother, Stephie broke into fresh sobbing. "I just wanted to see Harley, Mama. But I fell in the creek. I'm so cold," she wailed pitifully.

Mary Claire hugged her daughter and cried along with her. "It's okay, baby. Shh. It's okay. You're safe now. We'll get you into a nice hot bath and you'll feel much better." Turning, she hurried to the house without so much as a thank-you, leaving Harley and the other men sitting on their horses, watching them.

Cody saw the worry in Harley's eyes, the weight of guilt on his shoulders. He leaned over and gave his friend a pat on the back. "She'll be okay," he said by way of comfort. "A hot bath and a generous dose of mothering and she'll be fit as a fiddle by morning."

Harley never once moved his gaze from the figures retreating through the darkness. "It's my fault," he murmured. "All my fault."

Mary Claire tucked the covers securely beneath Stephie's chin, then stepped back, dragging a wrist beneath her eye to catch a lingering tear.

"She'll be okay," Leighanna whispered as she placed an arm around Mary Claire's shoulders.

Mary Claire leaned into her friend, tipping her head against Leighanna's. "I know," she murmured tearfully. "But I don't think I've ever been so frightened."

Leighanna inhaled deeply as she, too, stared down at Stephie, who was sleeping peacefully now. "Me, neither," she said on a shuddery sigh.

"To think what could have happened! If not for Harley—" Mary Claire whirled to face her friend, her hands pressed over her lips, her eyes wide and stricken. "I didn't even thank him," she said. "I just grabbed Stephie and ran."

"I'm sure he understands," Leighanna murmured.

Mary Claire waved away the reassurance. "No. I said awful things to him this afternoon. I told him it was all his fault." She grabbed Leighanna's hands and squeezed them. "I've got to go to him. I've got to apologize for the things I said. Will you keep an eye on the kids for me?"

"You know I will."

Mary Claire found him in the barn, hunkered down in the stall with the calf, holding the bucket while the calf nursed. This was where it had all started, she remembered, where she'd lost her heart to Harley on that day that seemed light-years in the past. Tears stung her eyes. She missed him. God, how she missed him.

Moving to the stall door, she called softly, "Harley?"

He spun on the balls of his feet at the sound of her voice, yanking the nipple from the calf's mouth. Then he was on his feet, tossing the bucket aside. "What's wrong?'' he asked, his voice rising in panic. ''Has something happened to Stephie?''

Tears clogged her throat at the sight of him, and Mary Claire could only shake her head. ''No, she's fine,'' she finally managed. When she saw his shoulders sag in relief, she realized how much he cared for Stephie. And realizing that increased her guilt for the things she'd said.

''I came to apologize for what I said this afternoon and to thank you for saving Stephie's life.''

Harley's cheeks flamed and he ducked his head. ''No apology necessary. You were right. Her running away was all my fault.''

Mary Claire stretched out a hand to him, wanting to reassure him, but he stood steadfast, remaining just out of reach. Slowly, she dropped her hand. ''No, it wasn't,'' she said miserably. ''And it was cruel of me to blame you.''

Harley kicked angrily at the hay on the floor, sending the calf scampering to the far corner of the stall. ''It *was* my fault,'' he argued, then turned to meet her gaze. The pain and the guilt she saw in the depths of his blue eyes nearly broke Mary Claire's heart. ''I built false hope in her, in all of you, and I'm sorry about that.''

What the look in his eyes hadn't accomplished, his words almost did. ''False hope?'' Mary Claire repeated, gripping her hands on the stall door to keep from falling. ''Is that what you call what we shared?''

Harley dragged off his hat and raked his fingers through his hair in frustration. ''Yes.''

Mary Claire knew he was lying. What they'd shared had been far from false. A man as honest and loving as Harley could never fake the emotions, the tenderness, he'd shown them all just to get her in bed. That he would say such a thing filled her with a burning anger.

"You're a coward, Harley Kerr."

Harley's head snapped up and he met her gaze, his own narrowed dangerously. But then his anger faded from his eyes. "Yeah," he said in defeat. "I guess I am. But I never meant to hurt you, Mary Claire. Not you or your kids."

She hadn't known that mere words could cut so deep. "I think what you meant to say," she said bitterly, "is that *you* don't want to be hurt again. Isn't that nearer to the truth?"

Her words hit a little too close to home and Harley's mouth thinned to a white line. "I lost a family once," he said, and stooped to pick up the bucket. "I don't think I'd survive losing another one."

"Lose us?" she cried in dismay. "How could you lose us?"

He slapped the bucket's handle over a post and wheeled on her. "I heard you on the phone when you were talking to that *friend* of yours in Houston," he said, placing enough inflection on the word that Mary Claire realized he'd thought she'd been talking to a man. "I heard you say you'd give some thought to moving back to Houston. I also heard you say, 'I love you.'"

Mary Claire trembled with the injustice of it all. That he would take a conversation and let it ruin everything they had without asking for an explanation galled her no end. "That *friend* you refer to is Leigh-anna Farrow, and she's at my house right now keeping an eye on Stephie and Jimmy for me. And as far as telling her I'd give moving back to Houston some thought, it was just something to say. I have no intention of moving back to Houston or anywhere else. Temptation is our home.''

Though her explanation surprised Harley and shamed him a little, his resolve didn't once waver. The memory of Stephie clinging to that tree with the raging water sucking at her and knowing he was the cause of her being there was too much to bear. He couldn't let his heart get involved again. Loving hurt too damn much.

''It's no good, Mary Claire,'' he said, shaking his head. ''It would be better if we left things as they are. I can't get involved with y'all again.''

''Can't or won't?''

''Damn it, Mary Claire!'' he, roared. ''Can't you understand how much I lost, how much it hurt when I lost my wife and my children? You have no idea how painful that is.''

Mary Claire dropped her hands from the stall door and took a step back as if he'd slapped her. ''Don't I?'' she asked, her eyes burning with challenge. ''Do you think you hold the market on suffering? You forget, Harley, that I've gone through a divorce, too. And just because I'm the one who wanted the divorce doesn't mean that it didn't hurt.'' She curled her hands into tight fists at her sides. ''I loved Pete. I loved our children and the life we'd created together. But Pete couldn't be satisfied with one woman. He had to have them all. Do *you* realize how much that hurts? To know that your husband is with another woman and you can't do a damn thing about it?

"I never meant to fall in love with you, Harley. Like you, I was scared to open my heart again." She stiffened her shoulders, keeping her gaze level on his. "But you know what, Harley? With you, I was willing to take that chance."

Before he could respond, she turned and stormed from the barn and headed toward her van.

Nine

That, night, after Mary Claire left, Harley lay in bed, his hands laced beneath his head, his gaze fixed on the ceiling overhead. The extra pillow he usually found comfort in lay crumpled against the far wall where he'd tossed it.

I never meant to fall in love with you, Harley. Like you, I was scared to open my heart again. But with you, I was willing to take that chance.

Harley groaned and pushed himself to a sitting position, squeezing his fists against his eyes, trying to shut Mary Claire's words out of his mind. But they continued to stab at his conscience and his heart until he fell back against the headboard with a frustrated sigh.

You're a coward, Harley Kerr.

His body tensed in defense at the remembrance of

her accusation. He'd been called a lot of things in his life, but never a coward. In fact, most folks around Temptation considered him brave, something of a legend. At the tender age of seventeen, when his father had died, he'd taken on a man's responsibilities and run the ranch on his own, making it grow and prosper beyond even his father's wildest dreams. Along with the ranch, he'd accepted the guardianship of his stepsister, and though she'd eventually run away, taking with her a little of his heart, no one blamed Harley for her actions. Instead, they'd blamed his wife—and rightfully so. Susan had never liked his stepsister, even resented her presence in their home. She'd all but pushed the girl out the door.

And then he'd lost his family, and there were those who were sure that Harley would finally admit defeat and crawl away into some hole. But he hadn't. He'd flung himself even deeper into his work on the ranch, took what time his children would give him and slowly healed his heart, sealing it off from future pain.

And just when he thought he had everything under control, along came Mary Claire and her kids, and damn if he hadn't lost his heart to the lot of them— and run like a scared rabbit when he'd thought he was about to lose them all.

She was right. He was a coward. A yellow-bellied, stinking coward.

And Mary Claire Reynolds was the bravest woman he'd ever met. Any woman who would pack up her kids and go live in a town where she knew no one, move into a run-down house and turn it into a home and do all this with no means of support just to keep her kids safe had to be.

If she's willing to take a chance on you, can you do any less?

The question came out of nowhere, catching him off guard. Could he gamble his heart again? he asked himself, then rolled his eyes at the ceiling and cursed his own stupidity. Hell, his heart was already lost. What more did he have to lose?

He jackknifed from bed and stalked from his room as naked as the day he was born. In the laundry room, he pulled his jeans from the dryer and tugged them on.

Mary Claire Reynolds wasn't the only one willing to take a chance. Harley Kerr was willing to take a few of his own.

With his roan saddled and waiting, Harley stepped into the mare's stall. The sorrel tossed her head and backed away from him.

"Whoa, girl," he murmured soothingly, holding out his hand for her to sniff. She watched him from the corner of her eye, and when he didn't seem to pose a threat, she slowly moved toward him, pressing her velvet muzzle against the palm of his hand.

"We've got some convincing to do," he said as he slipped the halter over her nose and buckled it behind her ears. He gave those ears a scratch. "Think you can help me?"

She tossed her head and nickered. Harley chuckled ruefully as he led her from the stall, knowing they both had their work cut out for them.

The night was ripe with the smell of summer as Harley guided his roan with the sorrel mare in tow along the gravel drive to Mary Claire's. The only sound in the darkness came from the clattering of horses's hooves on the loose stones. A soft breeze stirred the honeysuckle planted along the low picket fence that surrounded her house and carried its sweet flowery scent to Harley's nose. He paused, inhaling deeply of it, thinking of the woman who'd planted it and the courage and determination she'd shown to carve a home for herself and her children in a two-bit town like Temptation. He thought, too, of his own cowardice. Sighing, he urged his horse on.

He stopped at the picket fence and swung down from the saddle. After tethering his horse, he un-wound the lead rope and quietly led the mare through the narrow gate. Beneath Mary Claire's bedroom win-dow, he stopped and looked up, his heart thudding against the wall of his chest. The lace panels fluttered beyond the open window in the breeze. Was he too late? he worried silently. Would she still be willing to take a chance on him?

Unwilling to give his fears time to bloom, he bent and scooped some pebbles from the ground and tossed them at the screen. Holding his breath, he waited. After what seemed like an eternity, he saw a shadow move between the lace panels.

"Mary Claire?" he called.

The shadow stepped closer to the window. "Har-ley? Is that you?"

"Yeah," he said, his voice husky with nervous-ness. "It's me. Can you come down for a minute?"

She hesitated so long he was sure she was going to refuse. Then her voice came softly, drifting down to him as it had so many times in the past, like the brush of velvet against his flesh. "Yes. Wait there."

His heart in his throat, Harley led the mare to the porch steps. Mary Claire slipped through the screen door, letting the door close quietly behind her. She stepped into the beam of moonlight, the hem of her nightgown whispering around her bare feet. When she reached the edge of the porch, she stopped and folded her arms protectively beneath her breasts.

She shifted her gaze suspiciously to the mare, then back to Harley. "What do you want?"

If there was a chill in her voice, Harley ignored it. "Well," he began hesitantly, wondering if it might not be wiser just to drop to his knees and beg, "I know it's not Christmas, but when I was in San Antonio a couple of weeks ago, I saw this mare here." he said. He lifted a hand to the animal's head and rubbed the white blaze that ran down her nose. "Her coat's almost the same color as your hair, and when I saw her, I thought of you. She seemed so proud standing there in the ring, but at the same time so alone."

He shook his head, letting his hand fall to his side as he dropped his gaze to his boots. "I didn't go to the auction to buy anything, but when I saw her, I remembered your telling me about always asking Santa for a horse, and then how disappointed you were when you didn't find one in the backyard Christmas morning." He found the courage to look at Mary Claire again and thought he saw the glimmer of tears in her eyes. "I know you aren't a little girl anymore, and you probably gave up on Santa ever giving you that horse years ago. But I wanted you to have her. I wanted to be the one to give you your dreams.''

Taking a chance, he held out the mare's lead rope to her.

Mary Claire started to move forward, then stopped and knotted her hands together at her waist. He saw the battle going on and prayed she'd take that first step.

When she didn't, he moved nearer, halting just shy of the foot of the steps. "She's gentle," he added, "though she hasn't been ridden in a while. Like me, she might be a little slow to take to a bit again.''

"Why, Harley?" she asked, her voice sounding raw in the quiet night. "Why are you doing this?''

He shifted from one foot to the other and dropped his gaze to the ground again. "Because I love you, Mary Claire.''

At her sharp intake of breath, he looked back up, his gaze colliding and locking with hers. The shock in her eyes, the utter pain behind it, tore at his heart. "I know that probably comes as a surprise to you after all I've put you through. But it's the truth. I swear.''

Drawing that final ounce of courage, he held out his other hand. He saw the tremble in her fingers, a sign of the battle that continued to wage in her. But he kept his hand extended, offering to her with his eyes so much more than just a simple hand down the steps.

When she continued to hesitate, he knew he had to go for broke, gambling all that he'd held close for so many years. "I want you to marry me, Mary Claire," he said, his voice husky with emotion. "If you will,

I promise to always love you, both you and your kids, and keep you safe from harm.''

Slowly her hands unknotted. Slower still, she reached out and slipped her quivering hand into his. Sighing his relief, he closed his fingers around hers and squeezed. ''Oh, God, Mary Claire,'' he murmured. ''I was so afraid I'd be too late.''

She flew down the steps that separated them and he dropped the lead rope to catch her in his arms. Holding her tight against his chest, he covered her face with his lips, kissing away the salty tears that leaked from her eyes.

''I'm sorry, baby, so sorry for being such a coward.''

She lifted her hands to cup his cheeks, then tipped his head back. The trembling smile the moonlight revealed on her face stole what was left of his heart.

''Don't be,'' she whispered as she looked lovingly into his eyes. ''You're here now. And that's what counts.''

He caught her hands in his and pressed a kiss into first one palm, then the other. A velvet snout bumped against his back, knocking him hard against Mary Claire. Laughing, he sidestepped, and the mare moved closer, thrusting her nose at Mary Claire.

A smile of the purest delight spread across Mary Claire's features, and she lifted her hand to stroke the mare's white blaze. ''You didn't have to buy me a horse to convince me to marry you. You know that, don't you?''

Harley chuckled. ''Figured it couldn't hurt.''

Laughing, Mary Claire looped her arm through his,

hugging him to her side, then turned to look at the mare again. "What's her name?"

Harley thought for a moment, watching the woman he loved bond with the horse who'd served him so well tonight. "Cupid," he said softly. "Her name's Cupid."

*   *   *   *   *

Hank Braden gets more then he expected when he hires Leighanna Farrow as the End of the Road's newest waitress in
A LITTLE TEXAS TWO-STEP
(SD#1090. 8/97), the second book of
Peggy Moreland's
TROUBLE IN TEXAS miniseries.
So come on back to Temptation, Texas...
and watch the sparks fly!!

Bestselling author

JOAN JOHNSTON

continues her wildly popular miniseries with an
all-new, longer-length novel

The Virgin Groom

HAWK'S WAY

One minute, Mac Macready was a living legend in
Texas—every kid's idol, every man's envy, every
woman's fantasy. The next, his fiancée dumped him,
his career was hanging in the balance and his future
was looking mighty uncertain. Then there was the
matter of his scandalous secret, which didn't stand a
chance of staying a secret. So would he succumb to
Jewel Whitelaw's shocking proposal—or take cold
showers for the rest of the long, hot summer…?

Available August 1997
wherever Silhouette books are sold.

Silhouette®

Take 4 bestselling love stories FREE

Plus get a FREE surprise gift!

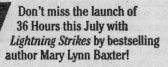

Silhouette makes it easy to heat up those long summer nights!

Clip the attached coupon and receive 50¢ off the purchase of *Hawk's Way: The Virgin Groom* by bestselling author Joan Johnston!

Available August 1997, wherever Silhouette books are sold.

SILHOUETTE® Desire®

COMING NEXT MONTH

#1087 NOBODY'S PRINCESS—Jennifer Greene
Alex Brennan, August's *Man of the Month*, was a white knight looking for a fair maiden to love. Regan Stuart was a beauty who needed someone to awaken her sleeping desires...and Alex was more than willing to rescue this damsel in distress.

#1088 TEXAS GLORY—Joan Elliott Pickart
Family Men
Posing as sexy Bram Bishop's wife was the closest to marriage headstrong Glory Carson ever wanted to come. But it didn't take much acting to pretend that the most wanted bachelor in Texas was the prince of her dreams.

#1089 ANYBODY'S DAD— Amy Fetzer
Mother-to-be Tessa Lightfoot's solo baby parenting plans didn't include Chase Madison, the unsuspecting sperm bank daddy. But if Tessa didn't keep him out of her life, she didn't know how much longer she could keep him out of her bed.

#1090 A LITTLE TEXAS TWO-STEP—Peggy Moreland
Trouble in Texas
Leighanna Farrow wanted a home, a family and a man who believed in happily-ever-after. Hank Braden wanted Leighanna. Now, the sexiest, most confirmed bachelor in Temptation, Texas, was about to learn what this marriage business was all about....

#1091 THE HONEYMOON HOUSE—Patty Salier
For better or worse, Danielle Ford had to share close quarters with her brazenly male colleague, Paul Richards. And his sizzling overtures were driving her to dream of her own honeymoon house.

#1092 UNEXPECTED FATHER—Kelly Jamison
Jordan McClennon was used to getting what he wanted, and he wanted former flame Hannah Brewster and the little boy he thought was their son. But when the truth came out, would it change how he felt about this ready-made family?